FROMAGE TO ETERNITY

THE STRANDED IN PROVENCE MYSTERIES
BOOK 10

SUSAN KIERNAN-LEWIS

SAN MARCO PRESS

Fromage to Eternity. Book 10 of The Stranded in Provence Mysteries.

Copyright © 2024 by Susan Kiernan-Lewis

All rights reserved.

Books by Susan Kiernan-Lewis

The Maggie Newberry Mysteries

Murder in the South of France

Murder à la Carte

Murder in Provence

Murder in Paris

Murder in Aix

Murder in Nice

Murder in the Latin Quarter

Murder in the Abbey

Murder in the Bistro

Murder in Cannes

Murder in Grenoble

Murder in the Vineyard

Murder in Arles

Murder in Marseille

Murder in St-Rémy

Murder à la Mode

Murder in Avignon

Murder in the Lavender

Murder in Mont St-Michel

Murder in the Village

Murder in St-Tropez

Murder in Grasse

Murder in Monaco

Murder in Montmartre

Murder in the Villa

A Provençal Christmas: A Short Story

A Thanksgiving in Provence

Laurent's Kitchen

The Claire Baskerville Mysteries

Déjà Dead
Death by Cliché
Dying to be French
Ménage à Murder
Killing it in Paris
Murder Flambé
Deadly Faux Pas
Toujours Dead
Murder in the Christmas Market
Deadly Adieu
Murdering Madeleine
Murder Carte Blanche
Death à la Drumstick

The Savannah Time Travel Mysteries
Killing Time in Georgia
Scarlett Must Die
The Cottonmouth Club

The Stranded in Provence Mysteries
Parlez-Vous Murder?
Crime and Croissants
Accent on Murder
A Bad Éclair Day
Croak, Monsieur!
Death du Jour
Murder Très Gauche
Wined and Died
Murder, Voila!
A French Country Christmas
Fromage to Eternity

The Irish End Games

Free Falling
Going Gone
Heading Home
Blind Sided
Rising Tides
Cold Comfort
Never Never
Wit's End
Dead On
White Out
Black Out
End Game

The Mia Kazmaroff Mysteries
Reckless
Shameless
Breathless
Heartless
Clueless
Ruthless

Ella Out of Time
Swept Away
Carried Away
Stolen Away

1

I know this might sound corny, but I've decided that newlywed life is not so different from a movie of the nineteen forties. I've discovered that this stage of one's life is all studied glances, champagne coupes and blushes. Take now for instance. I was walking along a sunset-drenched vineyard, my hand entwined with my husband's—not unlike the bursting grapevines all around us. The air was thick with the scent of lavender and ripening grapes.

I sighed and stole a glance at Luc who seemed enthralled with the view of the aforementioned sunset-drenched fields. He was so gorgeous that I had to pinch myself to remind myself that I wasn't dreaming and that he really was mine.

Honestly, any minute now cartoon bluebirds were going to start flitting about my head. It was all so perfect, that it was almost impossible to grasp that this was really my life now. Me, deliriously happy living in a place where every stone was steeped in history and every sunset was a brand-new revelation. With this sexy Frenchman.

"*Regarde*," Luc said, pointing to the horizon where the

sky was busy painting itself in hues of pink and orange to complete the picture of my perfect life. "*C'est magnifique, n'est-ce pas?*"

I gave his hand a squeeze. It *was* magnificent. All of it. Especially when you added the fact that I was finally and completely married—two months now. And when you consider how I originally came to Provence—alone, heartbroken, and recently dumped by my boyfriend, mere seconds before a dirty bomb ignited over the Mediterranean Sea, throwing me and the rest of Europe back to the eighteen hundreds—well, my little sun-drenched walk in the park tonight is nothing short of a miracle.

It sounds pretty romantic when I look at it in retrospect like that. But, at the time, it was the most traumatic thing that had ever happened to me. I didn't speak French—still don't if you ask my friends. I didn't know anyone in this country, I didn't have a permanent to place to live, and I had no idea what was happening back in the States where I'm from.

Fortunately, over the past three years most of that has gotten sorted. I found out that someone back in the US adopted my cat—my main worry. And I learned that I can handle just about anything that's thrown at me. It had taken three long and painful years before my country began rounding up all of us expats stranded in various points of the world—and by then I was no longer in the mood to go home.

By then I'd made a life for myself here. I'd made friends. I'd made a home and a business. I'd met Luc. I'd started to learn the language. If you'd have told me two years ago when the opportunity came to go home that I'd take a pass on it, I'd have never believed you. Make no mistake. Life is hard here. I have to collect firewood to make a cup of tea.

After the EMP blitzed all electronics, I've had to live without cars, trains, planes, and telephones. And worse, the Internet. Can you imagine? Literally everything I do, I do the hard way.

I have the occasional use of a horse to help me get from village to village when that's necessary. Before I came to Provence and got stuck here in this foreign hinterland, clothing and fashion had been a major interest of mine. Now that washers and dry cleaners are a thing of the past, I wear the same thing day in and day out and cleanliness is no longer an assumed characteristic of my wardrobe. It's just too much trouble when other things are more important.

The bottom line to all this is to say that I've changed. After the EMP, we've all changed. But I've *really* changed.

"We should get back," Luc said, tugging me in the direction of his cottage.

He had a smile in his voice when he said it, and I could tell his desire to return home had less to do with the darkening skies and wanting his dinner than it did his wanting to be alone with me behind a door that locked.

"I'll race you," I said with a laugh before we both took off in a mad rush back to our proverbial love nest.

The next morning, I slipped out of bed and padded to the kitchen, intent on crafting a breakfast befitting a partner who was my anchor and sail in equal measure. (Have I mentioned how much I'm enjoying being married?) As I whisked eggs and sliced the tomatoes that I'd gathered the day before from a friend's garden, it occurred to me that Luc was possibly more anchor than sail. Truth be told, an anchor was often what I needed most. I have a tendency to jump first and interpret the situation for signs of disaster later. That formula has not always worked out for me. In contrast, Luc is a much more analytical person and that's been a good blend.

Plus, I have to say the cultural divide between us has always been fascinating to me—and very sexy. Luc is French to the bone and it's not just his accent that constantly reminds me of that. He regularly attempts to curb me from doing or saying things that any normal American boyfriend would simply have accepted. I find that tendency adorable and so different from what I'm used to. In some ways, being with him is like living with a real-life Regency Alpha male.

As our village chief of police, Luc is definitely a study in contrasts. Stern and by-the-book. But also easygoing and susceptible. Of course, there are times when I find his strict adherence to the rule of the law a bit much. He does have a tendency to dictate rather than advise, but that was most present when we were just dating or hanging out. The real tenor of our marriage is early days yet.

Now that we were joined at the hip, he couldn't just slam a door and ghost me for a week if he was frustrated with me and my American ways. Now that we'd finally committed to each other, there was plenty of time to gently blend our styles and for me to learn how to corral his up-to-now sexy if dictatorial tendencies.

"Something smells wonderful," Luc said from the doorway. I turned to see him leaning against the frame, tousled hair casting shadows over his green eyes. Have I mentioned that Luc is seriously handsome? Best of all, he doesn't seem to know it.

"*Omelette aux herbes*," I said, flipping the omelet before noticing that the fire had gone out on the stove.

I've made omelets many times during the years I lived

with *les soeurs*—the ninety-five-year-old twin sisters who'd been my roommates up until I married Luc two months ago. They tended to do most of the cooking but had always insisted that I have at least one dish under my belt in case they both came down with the flu at the same time. They taught me that there's something sacred about preparing food for people you love. Until the twins, I'd never experienced that.

Luc came into the kitchen and slipped his arms around me, trapping me at the stove. I leaned into him, letting the omelet sputter in the pan for a moment.

"*Je t'aime*, Jules," he murmured into my hair.

"*Je t'aime* you too," I said turning in his arms. "But your breakfast will burn."

He kissed me then. I could tell he was struggling with whether to go to work hungry or happy. In the end, he released me. As he seated himself at the table so I could plate his omelet and pour his coffee, I felt so domesticated that I seriously regretted not being able to chronical the moment on Instagram.

"*C'est delicieux*, Jules," he said as he bit into his omelet. "Where is your breakfast?"

"I'll have mine when you leave," I said as I fondly watched him eat.

It's true that Luc and I have had some serious ups and downs in the three years we've known each other. Because our attraction was so immediate, we'd had to walk away from the relationship at least twice before we finally put our mutually stubborn inclinations on a shelf and allowed ourselves to commit to each other. It's been a long road but one I'm grateful beyond reason we finally allowed ourselves to go down.

I sat next to him at the table. Truthfully, I wasn't eating

because there had only been enough eggs for one omelet. But I didn't mind. I wasn't hungry at the moment, and if I got hungry later, I'd just head over to *La Fleurette*, the twelfth-century carriage house where I used to live with *les soeurs*. There was always something on the stove there.

"What's your day look like?" I asked as I sipped my coffee—already cold and of course now that the fire had gone out, there was no easy way to reheat it.

He cut into his omelet and shrugged.

"No open cases," he said. "Probably just paperwork. I might go over to the mayor's office and talk with Katrine."

Katrine Pelletier was an old friend of mine—well, three years old. She'd won the mayoral election the year before. She was also a single mother of two small children. Between her job and her single mother status, she was stressed a lot.

"Something going on there?" I asked.

"No, no. When we have a slow period, I just like to hear any issues she might have. Keep ahead of it."

"Smart."

Luc is like a lot of men I know in that he doesn't talk very much and certainly not at length. Me, I'm a talker. On top of that, I've got a reporter's inclination—probably because that's what I used to be back in Atlanta before I came to Provence. Since I don't speak the language here well enough for journalism to be an occupational option for me, I have turned my natural curiosity to investigative and private detective work. I find the nature of the business suits me and the way my mind works. Plus, it's never boring. I am painfully aware that Luc isn't crazy about me doing investigative work, which is disappointing, but there you have it. Already two months old and already our marriage isn't perfect.

"And what does your day look like?" he asked as he

finished his omelet with a swig of cold coffee and a quick expression of distaste he nearly managed to hide from me.

"I'll probably go over to *La Fleurette*," I said. "And see if the twins need me for anything."

"Of course," he said and then took a breath.

It's true that I haven't been married to Luc long but I've known him long enough to know when something is on his mind. The intake of breath and then nothing was a tell that I was familiar with. I've learned to wait for it though. Asking him what's on his mind only tends to slow down his process.

"We probably should start weeding the garden," he said finally. "It's nearly summer."

"Good idea," I said, although I knew very well that by *we* he meant *me*.

After that he left the table to finish dressing for work and I picked up his dish and our mugs and put them in the sink. Because we don't have hot water heaters anymore, I'll have to heat up a container of water before cleaning the breakfast dishes. And to do that, I'll have to first build a fire.

A few minutes later, as I was coaxing a flame from the sticks jammed in the fire box on the stove in order to heat up the dishwashing water, Luc kissed me goodbye and set out for his day. Our cottage was only a half mile from the village of Chabanel where he works, but he always drove there in his 2013 Citroen Hatchback. He is one of only two people in the area who has a working car but of course as chief of police he needed one.

As I watched him drive off, I found myself deliberately extinguishing the budding flame I'd created as the thought occurred to me that I could just head over to *La Fleurette* and get a cup of hot coffee which seemed an imminently more sensible way to start my day.

2

Luc entered the village police station, breathing in the familiar scents of old wood, stale coffee, and paperwork. Even in broad day light, the front office although neat and orderly, was dimly lit with only a few electric lamps providing illumination.

The front reception area was empty. Madame Gabin was late coming in again. Luc had noticed that she had started coming in later and later ever since he'd married. He stepped down the hall leading to the holding cells in the back which were dark and forbidding, their metal bars glinting in the low light.

Even Matteo wasn't in yet. They'd had another detective, Eloise, but she'd had some long-brewing issues with Jules so that when she'd asked to transfer to Lyons Luc had been only too glad to see her go. Unfortunately, that meant he and Matteo were shorthanded until her replacement came.

As Luc made his way down the hall to his office, his stomach rumbled, reminding him he'd had only a meagre breakfast. Jules had been so proud of the omelet she'd made him this morning that he didn't have the heart to tell her it wasn't nearly enough for him. He glanced at the files stacked on his desk as he walked into his office. Things were quiet. He'd head out for an early lunch at the café to make up for the paltry breakfast.

He knew Jules was doing her best. Just seeing the effort that she went to for him filled his heart with love for her. He was hoping to ask Madame Gabin if she would give Jules knitting lessons. He'd been astonished to hear that she didn't know how to knit or sew. Probably the American in her didn't consider either a viable skill worth learning. It was a surprise to him that *les soeurs* hadn't taught her when they were living together. They probably figured it was more trouble than just doing it themselves.

He sat down at his desk and picked up one of the files from a case that was essentially resolved but not quite closed. It was a property dispute that Luc had successfully arbitrated—after one neighbor had paid a fine for assaulting the other. The two men had agreed to Luc's suggested terms and now all that was needed was the final closing report.

A sound in the other room prompted Luc to look up. He could smell the aroma of strong coffee and he found his mouth watering. Madame Gabin often brought coffee and pastries into work. He walked down the hall to the waiting room where her desk was. Sure enough, she had set two large cups of coffee on her desk.

"Good morning, Chief," she said. "One of those is yours."

"Appreciate it," Luc said, taking the coffee and realizing he couldn't scold her now for coming in late.

"And help yourself to the *pains aux raisins*," she said, indicating the bag on her desk.

Madame Gabin had worked as the village police station receptionist for over fifteen years. She was a gossipy woman in her late fifties, with a no-nonsense attitude but a veritable font of village information, some factual, some just mean-spirited. Her dark hair was shot through with silver and frown lines creased the downward tilt of her mouth.

"And how is married life this morning, Chief?" she asked, her lip curled into a subtle sneer.

Madame Gabin had never been a fan of Jules. Perhaps he'd rethink asking her to teach her how to knit.

"Same as yesterday morning," he said. "Perfection."

She snorted and began to sort out the files on her desktop as she got ready for her day. Luc fished out two *pains aux raisins* and returned to his office.

"Matteo?" he asked over his shoulder.

"I have no idea," she said.

Luc felt a shiver of annoyance. Their ongoing lack of cellphones was the main lingering consequence of the EMP which continued to negatively impact their lives in the village—and certainly his ability to do his job. There was a landline at Gabin's desk and an ancient car phone in Luc's car. Hardly ideal.

He sat back down at his desk and quickly ate the pastry but took his time with the coffee. He frowned at the stack of administrative work on his desk and found his attention wandering to the view out his window.

The sun's rays illuminated the golden hues of the ancient stone buildings of the village, casting shadows on the cobblestone street. A breeze carried the scent of the vineyards from the outskirts of town which mixed with the aroma of freshly baked bread from the nearby *boulangerie*.

It had only been two months since their simple yet beautiful wedding, but already Luc could sense a hint of discord developing with Jules. Their paths no longer crossed during their daily rounds as they had when they were dating. At home, silences seemed to grow where once they'd shared confidences. Was he imagining it? Had married life changed the close bond they'd once had? They rarely talked about it, but often Jules came home after he did, exhausted and mentally immersed in whatever project she was working on—with no time to ask about his day.

He knew he made the situation worse by becoming impatient with her so-called work. He'd made it clear before they married that he didn't want her to continue to do private investigation work. He thought she'd understand without him having to come right out and tell her to quit. His few covert conversations with *les soeurs* about how to handle her had assured him that Jules was only stubborn and independent—the very traits he enjoyed about her. They urged him to believe that his continued patience was the best way around her.

But with each passing day, she seemed more solidly entrenched in her ways than ever.

And he was still eating herb omelets most evenings for dinner.

Shaking his head to dismiss unwelcome thoughts, he turned again to the stack of reports.

Where the hell is Matteo?

He would need to have a conversation with him. Especially now that they were short staffed, Matteo needed to be told that he couldn't take advantage of the changes at the station. And knowing Matteo, that's exactly what he'd do. Now more than ever, Luc needed him on time and ready to go the extra mile. Probably hopeless, Luc thought with irritation.

I have one detective and he is already trying to retire while collecting a full paycheck.

Luc felt a stiffness developing in his neck. He stood up,

suddenly too antsy to sit still. He was hungry. The pastries hadn't filled him up. Maybe he'd do a walking circuit around the village square and try to walk off a little of the energy and restlessness that seemed to be vibrating through him. Then he'd go to lunch. Maybe even have a glass of wine.

As he came to Madame Gabin's desk he stopped when he saw she was on the phone.

"He's here right now," she said into the phone. "It's Matteo," she said to Luc.

Luc frowned and held out his hand for the phone.

"Yes?" Luc said into the phone.

"I'm at the *boulangerie*," Matteo said. "I did my rounds this morning before coming in and had two people say there was something strange going on at the cheese seller's shop."

"Strange how?"

"Nobody's seen the owner Hélo Montrachet in two days. Hasn't opened the shop."

"Maybe he's away."

"Witnesses say he never goes anywhere. He has no family."

"Stay put. I'll be right there."

He handed the phone back to Madame Gabin.

"Everything okay?" she asked.

"That's what I intend to find out," he said as he turned toward the door and headed into the beautiful spring morning.

3

That morning, I decided to ride my bike to *La Fleurette* which is three miles from the village of Chabanel and two miles from Luc's cottage. The house sits on a small rise surrounded by fields, along with a manicured *potager* and an ancient stone wall encircling the property. Honeysuckle and lavender run riot on the perimeter of the small front porch that lines the half-moon drive in front of the house.

When I was still about a quarter mile from the house, I could hear my dog Cocoa barking. I assumed the twins had her penned up inside or she would've come out in the road to greet me. When I pulled up to the house, I parked my bike on the front stoop and looked up at its presentation, amazed.

Even though it was only mid-May, the twins had already crammed every window top and bottom—five in all—with boxes of red geraniums. The hedges of purple and blue hydrangea were in full bloom too, flanking the large double wooden door. Seeing all the flowers reminded me that I was way behind schedule for doing anything with the garden at

Luc's—I mean, at *our* place. Luc wasn't the only one nagging me to do something with the garden. There hasn't been a single time I've seen *les soeurs* that they haven't asked me about my progress with it. Justine has even offered to come over to get me started. Ugh. I'm all for fresh spices and herbs at your fingertips but I suppose I'm still longing for the day that the stupid apocalypse is over and I am able to buy all that stuff at the grocery store like a normal person.

As soon as I opened the front door, Cocoa launched herself into my arms and immediately covered my face with sloppy dog kisses. I missed having her with me and I could see she missed me, too.

"Jules?" Justine called from the kitchen.

I put Cocoa down and closed the door behind me. The rooms inside *La Fleurette* are large—which is unusual for such an old *mas*—with high ceilings. The floors are scuffed stone slabs that have been here for generations. There's a massive fireplace mantel carved from a single stone that dominates the main hall. A wooden staircase leads to the upper floors, each of the steps wavy and uneven from hundreds of years of use.

"It's me," I said. "Any coffee still hot?"

Justine came out of the kitchen wiping her hands on a hand towel that was tucked into her belt. She had her white hair tied back off her face in a worn kerchief and was wearing an old apron or *tablier* over her day dress. I find Justine absolutely beautiful in spite of her age. She had married many decades ago and her husband had been deceased for years. Her twin sister Lèa on the other hand had never married and, if you knew her like I do, you'd be incredibly impressed with her strength, her bravery and her natural intuition. But you would not be surprised that she'd never married. She's prickly at the best of times.

In any event, they were both single now, in their midnineties, and both veterans of the French Resistance during the last world war. The two of them hold a high place of honor in Chabanel for their bravery and their valorous actions during the war. There weren't many of their kind left —even fewer as the years went by.

"Yes, *chérie*, there is coffee," Justine said, grinning with obvious delight to see me. "You did not bring Luc?"

"He's at work," I said as I made my way toward her to give her a kiss before moving into the kitchen where I could smell the coffee on the stove. The kitchen at *La Fleurette* was typical for the time when it was built. This room was the center of the house since food was then as it is now the center of every Frenchman's universe. The floor and walls were made of stone, great for keeping heat in, When the stove was hot it kept the whole house warm in winter and unbearable in summer. Our friend Thibault Theroux is incredibly handy cobbling together working electronics out of virtually nothing. He fashioned the large wood-fire oven at *La Fleurette*. There's also a refrigerator in the kitchen although of course it no longer works. The twins use it to store pantry items.

I brought down an earthenware mug and poured my coffee from the French press on the stove. A plate of croissants was on the kitchen table, and I helped myself to one. Just then Lèa came into the kitchen and cleared her throat.

"I don't suppose you are here to clean out the horse's stall," she said with a frown. "After finding Roulette wandering the countryside without his halter, Monsieur Dellaux is not happy."

I borrowed Monsieur Dellaux's horse Roulette when I needed to get from one place to another. We often kept him in a stall here at *La Fleurette,* but it had been over a week since I'd ridden him.

"Bonjour, Lèa," I said. "I thought Roulette was over at Monsieur Dellaux's place."

"Jules has come to visit with us," Justine said to Lèa as she poured herself a cup of coffee.

"And obviously to drink coffee," Lèa said pointedly.

"I don't know what you've been doing with *your* morning," I said to Lèa, "but I've already weeded both the garden, the *potager* and cleaned the kitchen floor over at Luc's."

All lies of course. But it pleased me to see Lèa's eyebrows jump up in surprise. She went to the open shelving over the stove and brought down a mug for herself, deciding I suppose that a visit was merited after all.

"I'm glad to see you are not embarrassing us by laying about and reading novels all day," she said. "I was sure you would. Come sit and tell us the news."

I know it sounds like she hates me or at the very least doesn't see the point of me, but Lèa Cazaly is actually quite fond of me. Dare I say, she loves me. But she's a prickly old hen and I've learned that one needs to get past the thorns to get to the cuddles.

Just kidding. There are no cuddles.

"Well, I made my special *omelette aux herbes* for Luc this morning before he went to work," I said.

Lèa snorted.

"You think you deserve praise for making your husband eggs for breakfast?"

"*Chérie*, didn't you make him that for dinner a few nights ago?" Justine asked gently.

"He likes it," I said defensively. "He said he can't eat it enough."

"He is just saying that to be polite," Justine said. "*Chérie*, you must learn to cook him something else."

"Why? If he wants something else, why can't he learn to cook it?" I asked. "Why is that my job?"

"I told you she would ruin this!" Lèa said to Justine, clucking her tongue and shaking her head at the same time.

"I'm not ruining anything," I said, feeling my face flush with annoyance. "Will you just butt out and let me and Luc do things our way?"

"You realize that we are Catholic and divorce is out of the question?" Lèa asked.

"Okay, I'm pretty sure even Catholics are allowed to divorce nowadays," I said, feeling a headache forming. "And Luc and I are not in trouble."

"Not yet," Justine said unhappily.

"Not at *all*," I stressed.

"But *chérie*," Justine said. "You did say you would try not to be so independent, didn't you?"

"I can't imagine I said anything of the kind," I said hotly. "And that's rich coming from you, Justine. I'm looking at two people who single-handedly took on the German army. As teenagers."

"You have been reading too many novels," Lèa said with a sniff.

"I might be exaggerating but I'm not wrong about you both being the very definition of independent when you were my age."

"I was married at your age," Justine reminded me. "And not at all independent."

"Well, I don't believe that," I said "You can't have changed that much with one simple marriage ceremony. I have a job and Luc knows and respects that."

Again, another lie. Why do I bother coming here if I have to fib about everything?

"Luc did not marry Hercules Poirot!" Lèa said. "He wants a wife!"

"And he's got one!" I said, raising my voice. "And trust me there are no complaints on his end!"

"Do not be crude, *chérie*," Justine admonished.

I looked at her in bewilderment although I suppose when you're her age and have lived your whole life communicating through euphemisms and metaphors instead of coming right out with what you mean, my *he's-got-no-complaints* line probably sounded lewd.

"Look," I said. "Everything is great between me and Luc. We're happy. It's great."

"But still no baby?" Lèa asked with a raised eyebrow.

Bracing myself in order not to throw my empty coffee mug at her, I set it down deliberately and forced myself to smile.

"We've only been married two months," I said slowly.

"Are you using protection?" Justine asked. "Because that would explain it."

I began to sputter in frustration, my headache now full-blown, when Lèa saved me from saying something I would be sorry for later.

"Enough," she said, finishing off her coffee and standing up. "We don't have all day for this."

Justine collected the coffee mugs and turned to the sink. I could see she already had a steaming pan of water on the stove for washing up.

"You will let us know when Luc finds the missing cheese seller?" she said over her shoulder as if deliberately not returning to the conversation of my inadequacies as a bride.

"The who?" I asked as I ruffled Cocoa's ears, holding

back the time when I would have to get back on my bike and head home to the cottage and its endless list of chores waiting for me.

"Monsieur Montrachet," Lèa said. "The man we buy our cheese from in Chabanel."

"He's missing?" I asked.

"Nobody has seen him," Justine said. "But I'm sure Luc will get to the bottom of it."

I felt a flash of envy that Luc was going to have a proper case to investigate. And not one he'd have to hide or justify investigating. No one was giving *him* a hard time for doing his work. While it was true that missing persons cases in Chabanel typically tended to be people wandering off drunk and falling in a ditch, they were always interesting to unravel.

"I'm sure he will," I said, feeling the bite of my envy deep in my core.

4

I spent the rest of the day cleaning and weeding the impossible *potager*, mostly so I wouldn't feel like such a liar after telling the twins that I'd done it. Fortunately, the garden patch wasn't too large, but it was still an overwhelming task for me. Everywhere I looked rogue vines clung to whatever they could, snaking across the soil and intertwining with the stems of other plants.

The once distinct borders of the plot were obscured by creeping ground cover, spilling onto the surrounding pavered pathway. Dandelions reared their yellow heads defiantly among the chaos making it at least easier to tell weed from possibly salvageable plant.

By the end of the afternoon, I was sweaty, dirty, and unable to really see much progress. Justine had snuck me a couple of pork chops before I left that she'd gotten from Thibault who got them through the black market, as well as a bag of rocket lettuce from the garden at *La Fleurette*.

By the time I'd washed and gotten the fire going for the chops, Luc was home from the station.

"You've made a good start in the *potager*," he said as he washed his hands in the sink.

I felt an annoyed prickle that I was being patronized. I made an effort to push the thought away. I'd spent the day digging in the dirt and trying to keep the fire going. *He'd* spent a productive day looking at clues, talking to people, interviewing witnesses, and then having lunch at the village café, all while his staff kowtowed to him.

He peered into the paper wrapping that held the two pork chops.

"Where did you get these?"

From the way he asked, it was clear he already knew where I'd gotten them. I don't know how. There was nothing obvious that shouted *black market*. At least not to me.

"I didn't get around to going to the *charcuterie* in town," I said, wondering why I was feeling like I'd done something wrong when all I'd wanted was to give him a nice dinner tonight.

"We cannot be taking food from *les soeurs*," he said with a frown.

I held my tongue. It's not true what they say. You don't get a big pat on the back when you stop yourself from snapping at an unappreciative spouse.

"How about wine?" I said, trying to make him smile even though I really felt like throttling him.

"Not wine, not pork chops," he said seriously.

When I didn't respond, he continued.

"You know that I cannot have my wife be seen to buy contraband from the black market. I know Thibault is a good friend of yours—"

"I'd have said he was a good friend of yours too."

I turned to face him and crossed my arms.

"Yes, of course," he said impatiently. "I'm just saying that

Thibault has a history of cutting corners on what he does, and as the wife of the village police chief—"

"Look, as much as I'd love to hear the rest of that sentence," I said, tossing down a dish towel, "and trust me, I'm dying to hear where it ends up, I'm afraid I'm working on a bit of a headache. Would you mind getting the grill going and putting the chops on? Thank you, *chérie*."

I turned and went to our bedroom, careful not to slam the door behind me.

Not surprisingly, dinner that night was quiet. Luc put the chops on the grill and even cleaned the rocket lettuce since I hadn't gotten around to doing it myself. I don't know whether he thought we'd gotten the greens from our own garden—an impossibility if he had eyes to see—or if I'd bought them in town, but he was wise enough not to ask me about them. Although I'd been half-joking about the wine, I have to admit, we could've used a bottle that night to smooth the rough edges off our little skirmish.

"Dinner was very good," he commented, I suppose in an attempt to be conciliatory. But since I'd gotten the dinner from *les soeurs* and was not responsible for its procurement or its preparation in any way, I'm not sure how he thought he was complimenting *me*. Maybe he was just speaking out loud and praising himself?

When the meal was done, I picked up both plates to bring them to the sink since it was only fair that I be the one to wash them—even though it would take me forever since we hadn't kept the fire going while we ate. I was in a sour mood and didn't trust myself not to say something I'd be sorry for, so I set about cleaning up in silence.

"I collected the mail today," Luc said. "There's a letter for you."

My eyes widened in surprise, and I turned and wiped my hands on a kitchen towel. He stood at the table with a letter in his hand. I was surprised that he hadn't given me the letter as soon as he got home. I held out my hand for it. But instead of handing it to me, he put it on the table.

"What the heck, Luc?" I said in annoyance as I went to the table and snatched it up.

Instantly I could see why he was acting weird. The letter was from a friend of mine, Davos Bellinort, an investigative historian who had come through Chabanel last year looking for stories for the new Paris Liberation Museum in Paris. Davos had been scouring the countryside for stories of Resistance fighters during the last world war, not just for the new museum but also for a book he was writing. He'd come to Chabanel because he'd heard about the twins and was hoping for an interview.

Because Justine and Lèa hadn't felt comfortable sitting down to talk with a stranger about what they'd done in the war, Davos had urged me to interview them to find the details of their stories. He said they would probably be eligible to receive the *Légion d'honneur*. And honestly, I wanted that for them. What they did during the war was a big deal. I wanted them to be recognized for it. After Davos had left town, I started interviewing the twins. In the meantime, I kept in touch with Davos for any tips as to what would be most impressive for the medals decision committee responsible for deciding who got the prestigious award.

"Why are you still writing this guy?" Luc asked frowning as I tucked the letter unopened into the pocket of my *tablier*.

I felt my neck begin to tense up at his tone.

"You know why," I said.

"Does he know you're married now?"

"He has no interest in me in that way," I said, trying to keep my tone level.

I was well aware that a simple vocal inflection could set the two of us down a rocky night of bickering.

"He's just interested in interviewing subjects for the book he's writing," I said.

"Sure, he is."

I have to say I find it profoundly frustrating that Luc was jealous of the guy who was helping me with my project of finding national recognition for the twins. Or, let's face it, just having a relationship of any kind with another man. It's true that Davos is good looking. I'm sure that doesn't help.

I did my best to shake off my pique. It wouldn't help for *both* of us to be pissed off.

"Look, Luc," I said. "We have a little Château d'Esclans left. Why don't I leave the dishes for later and we sit out and enjoy the evening?"

It was clear that Luc wasn't even tempted. I know how it feels not to be able to shake off a bad mood. I guess I'd hoped he'd try a little harder.

"I've got work to do," he said tightly.

"Oh?" I asked. "Anything interesting?"

"Just work."

"I heard about the missing cheese seller," I said. "What's going on there?"

He looked at me. "How did you hear about that?"

"Chabanel is a small village. You know how these things go. I heard about it from the twins. So what's going on? Did he run off or what?"

I cannot tell you the range of emotions that passed across Luc's face right then. I'd delivered my question in a lighthearted manner, so I was surprised when he stared at me as if I'd somehow thrown down a challenge to him.

"I think we need to get something straight between us," he said.

I felt my back stiffen. As sure as anything, I felt an ultimatum coming.

"My work will stay at the station," he said. "I will not bring it home at night and I don't want you asking me about it. Do you understand?"

I stared at him. It looked like I was wrong about the ultimatum. It was just a plain old bare bones insult.

"Completely," I said coldly.

The expression on my face must have finally gotten through to him because his expression softened. He came to me and pulled me into his arms.

"I'm sorry, *chérie*," he said. "I don't know why I said that. Of course, you can ask me about my day. Forgive me?"

We kissed and I felt the tension begin to melt in my shoulders.

"Only if you get the water hot for the dishes," I said with an arched eyebrow.

He grinned.

"It's the least I can do," he said.

5

The next morning, Luc was up and gone even earlier than usual. We'd miraculously managed to have a good evening last night after his apology. I hadn't managed to cobble together anything this morning for his breakfast since he left before I could even get the stove heated up for coffee. I knew he'd find both food and coffee in the village and I think it was a relief for both of us when he left without making me try to put something together here.

A soft drizzle this morning had given me a reprieve on working in the garden for which I was glad, but I also had a date in the village with Katrine that I'd been looking forward to all week. Since I didn't have the horse or access to a car and the weather wasn't conducive for walking, I decided to ride my bike. Unfortunately the ride to the village was very wet and bumpy. Now that most cars and other vehicles were largely a thing of the past, no one was interested in doing road repairs. As a result, all the roads were full of potholes and overgrown patches. I hunkered down under my rain slicker and made the two-mile trip to town in just under thirty minutes.

The Café Provençal in Chabanel was the main meeting place in the village even though it was just a few small bistro tables on what used to be a sidewalk. Ownership of the place had changed hands at least three times since the EMP had eliminated supply chains, electricity and most staffing but the villagers were always still keen to go there. They were French. Café life is not just a meme or a postcard saying. It's truly a way of life in France. Even during the apocalypse. I think the villagers would've hung out there even if there was no coffee or food which there fortunately usually was.

I stood with my bike at the corner of the terrace and scanned the café's diners. There was a table in the corner where two elderly women I didn't recognize were sharing gossip and keeping a watchful eye on the village street in front of them. Now that TV was a thing of the past, gossip and watching one's neighbors was more pervasive than ever.

An unsmiling waiter made his rounds, refilling coffees and chatting with customers. I spotted Katrine sitting by herself at a terrace table and reading the village newspaper. Although not given to wearing makeup or caring much about how she dressed, Katrine was a pretty woman with long wavy brown hair and blue eyes. I could imagine that she must have been a knockout when she was in her twenties. I always thought it a shame that she'd settled when she did. There was something about the way she sat there now, all alone, that made me a little sad and I don't know why. Katrine and I have had a bit of an up and down history in our friendship. We'd started out strong with an instant connection—it helped that she spoke English—but after a very unfortunate episode which involved her husband Gaultier getting shot in the spleen—an episode for which she might have every reason to believe I was responsible—well, things have never been the same between us.

While Gaultier survived his gunshot wound, he was currently serving a twenty-year prison sentence for reasons that had led up to why he was shot in the first place. The bottom line is that ever since he went away, life has been hard for Katrine, a single mother of two. I'm sure there are times when she looks at her life and wonders what it would have been like if I'd never come to Chabanel. She'd probably have her husband home for one thing.

I waved to her from the edge of the terrace before dropping my bike on the ground and hurrying over to her. We quickly cheek kissed and I saw that she'd already ordered a coffee for me.

"Just what I need," I said as I sat down. "Hot coffee and a good chat with you. How are the little ones?"

"Not so little," she said with a laugh. "But good."

"Is your mother minding them while you're at *la Mairie*?"

Her mother was nearly as difficult as Gaultier was duplicitous.

"No, that was not working," Katrine said with a sigh. I thought she looked tired. "I'm making enough now to afford help and it's healthier for all of us, trust me."

"How is work?" I asked. "The village running along smoothly?"

I remembered that Luc said he was going to meet with her the other day and wondered if he had.

"So far so good," she said. "We've got the annual *patisserie* contest coming up."

I made a face because two years ago one of the judges of the contest had turned up dead and one of the twins had been arrested for her murder. The village had skipped a year on the annual tradition, but I guess everyone was ready to try again.

"I know what you're thinking," Katrine said. "But it's a big annual draw for the village and Luc assured me there will be no murders to upset everyone."

"Ha ha," I said. "That Luc is such a card."

"Is everything okay?" she asked with a slight frown.

"Oh, yes, fine," I said. "You know how it is. First year marriage issues and all that."

I was about to ask her about her and Gaultier's first year of marriage but caught myself in time. People with husbands you've put in jail make things so awkward, you know?

"Like what?" she asked.

"Nothing major," I said. "Except I know he wishes I could cook and garden and maybe sew."

"You can learn those things."

"True, but the things that I like to do—*those* things he wishes I wouldn't do."

"You mean your private investigation work? I would've thought that would give you something more in common."

"I know. Right? But he hates me doing it. I literally tiptoe around him. I never feel comfortable bringing up any case I'm working on."

"Well, that's not good. But look, I'm sure he'll come around. Luc loves you."

"I'm just afraid he really loves the version of me he has in his head."

Katrine knit her brows together in a frown.

"Jules, that's ridiculous. If anyone knows you, it's Luc. He knows you love this work. He may be grumpy about it now, but he'll soften in time. Trust me, he wants you to be happy."

"Maybe he thinks I should want *him* to be happy."

"And I'm sure you do, but that doesn't mean giving up who you are."

"Thanks, Katrine," I said. "I feel better."

"Just continue to follow your heart and Luc will follow right behind you. This much I know."

She stretched out her hand and squeezed my hand and for just that moment at least, I really believed her.

6

After my coffee with Katrine—which really did me a world of good, I decided to pop in on Luc. I'd be lying if I said I wasn't hoping to grab some gossip from Madame Gabin about the missing cheese seller—or maybe from Luc himself. Katrine had made me feel after our coffee that all kinds of things were possible.

As I walked through the village toward the police station, I couldn't help but marvel at what seemed to me to be Chabanel's enduring spirit. Chabanel is nestled in the hills of Provence about twenty miles from the next biggest town, Aix-en-Provence. Despite the lack of modern conveniences like communications, electronics, cars, and electricity, everyone I saw on the street seemed content and at peace with their way of life.

The village's stone buildings and cobblestone alleys have literally stood guard over this valley for centuries, enduring all manner of changes from the outside world (including an EMP) and yet somehow preserving its timeless quality. And that was never truer than now.

Like most French villages, in the center of Chabanel was

an ancient church featuring a crumbling bell tower. There was also a war memorial next to the church to remind everyone of the history of the area and of the incredible sacrifices made by the forefathers—and mothers—of Chabanel.

I passed the *boulangerie,* which was second only to the café as being the most visited place in the village, and which has been providing the village with bread since 1832—although it probably didn't boast lesbian bakers back then like it does now. The Sunday produce market probably has more vendors than shoppers, but it never missed a beat when the EMP wiped out trucks and supply chains and still continues to provide on a daily basis everything any French person would need for a perfect meal in France: cheese, olives, honey, shellfish, vegetables and fruit.

As I approached the *place de la Maire* near where the village police *municipale* was located and where Luc worked, I was struck as I always am by how pretty the building was. A two-story golden limestone building with terra cotta roof tiles and dark green shutters capped by a double front door of glossy ebony and a French flag hanging over it. I always found it interesting to think that French police chiefs had worked from this building to solve crimes in Chabanel since the seventeen hundreds.

I stepped into the station waiting room and immediately faced the receptionist, Madame Gabin, who without doubt considered herself the police station gatekeeper. She looked up from her desk when I entered and grimaced.

This cranky old bat danced at my wedding two months ago but now was sitting there glowering at me as if that had never happened. I should've known she'd only come for the free oysters and champagne.

"Is the Chief in?" I asked pleasantly.

"I'll see if he's free," she said.

You'd think I'd be used to her crap by now. Or maybe I was just worn down by three years of putting up with it.

"Unless he's interviewing a suspect," I said cheerfully, breezing past her desk. "He's free for me."

Miracles upon miracles, she didn't try to stop me. As I'd often suspected, she was just trying to see what she could get away with. I went to Luc's closed door and knocked. I only waited a moment before I opened the door and walked in. Luc was sitting at his desk, up to his elbows in papers and folders. It was immediately clear that he really did need some kind of assistant—not just a surly gatekeeper.

"Hey, you," I said, stepping into his office.

A surprised smile spread across his face when he saw me.

"*Chérie*," he said. "I didn't know you were in town today."

"I had coffee with Katrine."

I leaned across the desktop and kissed him and then sat down in the chair opposite his desk.

"You'll be happy to know I'm hitting the *boulangerie* on my way home," I said.

"You can bake bread, too, you know," he pointed out. "It's only flour and yeast."

"Okay, great. Tell you what. You bake the bread this weekend since it's so easy, and I'll do it next time."

I know I spoke a little too sharply but honestly! I thought he'd be thrilled I was thinking about dinner, but instead he only thought there was still more I could do. I felt a slight tightness in my chest.

"Perhaps you can run by the *charcuterie*?" he suggested.

"Or maybe you could," I pointed out. "Since I'm on a bike and you have the car."

"Yes," he said pleasantly. "I could do that."

"Awesome," I said, standing up.

I felt like things were getting tense and it was without doubt going to be me that made the first snarky comment and I wanted to be gone before that happened. I gestured toward his desk.

"Any news on the missing cheese seller?"

"All sorted," he said, standing up and coming around the desk to take me into his arms. "You made my day dropping by like this."

It helped my mood a bit, too.

"I'm glad," I said. "I'm picking up bread for the twins too."

I'd been hoping to also bring them a little news in the way of what happened to the cheese seller, but they'd be happy to get the bread in any case. Luc kissed me and gave my arm a squeeze as if to signal that it was time for me to go. But maybe I imagined that.

7

There were six people queuing up inside the *boulangerie*, but since I spotted a good dozen *baguettes* in the racks behind where the proprietor stood at the counter, I wasn't worried. If the *baguettes* sold out before I got there, I could still see plenty of *boules* and *fougasse*—either of which would appease *les soeurs*.

When I'm out and about in the village people often ask me after *les soeurs*. Those two are absolute legends in this village for what they did as members of the French Resistance. A normal person, i.e. a non-French person, might reasonably think that was a couple million years ago. But in France, memories are long even if they're really your parents' or grandparents' memories. The fact was that the twins were revered across Provence for their brave actions during the war.

"*Bonjour*, Madame DeBray," the proprietor Marie Fournier sang out to me, reminding me and everyone else in the shop that I was now the wife of the police chief.

Interestingly, Marie Fournier, who runs the bakery with

her partner Enora Roche, is about as sour as a woman can be. It makes no sense to me. To be surrounded by all this sugar and custard filling? I've always thought her grumpy affect had to do with the fact that she had to be up at three every morning making bread and was then forced to go to sleep early every night while everyone else was out enjoying *apèros* and having a normal life.

I looked around for Enora Roche. She'd come to town as a judge in the village's annual pastry competition two years ago and stayed when love found her in the form of our cranky village baker. Or maybe the apocalypse just made lesbian hook ups harder to find without the Internet. In any case, she stayed on.

"*Bonjour*, Madame Fournier," I replied with a big smile. "Is Madame Roche not around today?"

Instantly, the baker's face stiffened, and I was sorry I'd said anything. The woman was peevish at best. Leave it to me to step in the middle of an unresolved marital dispute. Before the baker could snarl out some unnecessary explanation, or tell me to mind my own business, I leaned across the counter and put in my order for the bread—making it clear that half the order was for *les soeurs*.

Normally, my connection to the twins tended to smooth away most of the natural consequences of my American blundering. I watched Fournier's face to see if it was working this time, but she just swiveled away in her wheelchair to grab the bread. The wheelchair was new. Marie had only recently become disabled. In fact, she was moving and walking fine when I left for my honeymoon two months ago but when I got back she was in the wheelchair. I heard it was some kind of accident, but I didn't know the full story. I made a mental note to ask the twins when I saw them next.

I wondered why I hadn't heard the details of why

Fournier was in a wheelchair before now. You can't keep a secret in this town. Do the twins know? As I watched Madame Fournier bag up my purchases, it occurred to me that they might well know but were keeping it from me.

One thing those two had learned during the war was how to keep a secret. Sometimes that skill came in handy, like when it was one of *my* secrets I needed them to keep. But mostly it was just hugely annoying.

Then Fournier did something which totally surprised me. Even with no fewer than four people waiting in line behind me, she handed over my wrapped bread and waved away my money.

"So does your husband know what happened to Hèlo?" she asked and jerked her head in the direction of the street.

"The cheese seller?" I shrugged. "Luc said he's got it all sorted."

"So where is Hèlo?" a customer behind me asked.

I turned as if to answer her when another woman in line piped up.

"I talked to Detective Matteo," she said, "and he said the police don't have a clue where Hèlo is!"

"So he's still missing?" I asked.

"*Yes*, he's still missing," Marie Fournier said testily. "And the local police are clueless as to why."

"Someone should ask Hèlo's girlfriend," a woman said.

"Tch! It's worth your life if you try. She snapped at me in the market yesterday and I was in line in front of her!"

Another woman I'd only seen a few times in the village stepped out of line to confront me.

"Tell your husband we need to know what he's doing about it," she said with a raised eyebrow as if the lack of progress or communications was somehow my fault.

"I will talk to him," I said.

"Bah! She knows less than we do," another woman said derisively.

My cheeks began to burn. But I knew she was right. It sounded as if the police were completely baffled by the cheese seller's disappearance.

Which was the opposite of what Luc had just told me.

I took my bread purchases and wound my way through the back of the line to the outside of the shop, keeping my head down and feeling a growing displeasure with Luc for putting me in this situation.

If he had no clue, all he had to do was say so! I'm his wife! I'm the one he's supposed to be honest with.

I stood for a moment on the sidewalk and let my feelings of vexation wash over me and as I did, I noticed movement out of the corner of my eye. Looking up I realized that the shop across the street had a wide red police tape across its door. It was the cheese seller's shop.

Standing in front of it with a key in his hand was none other than Detective Adrien Matteo. I watched as Matteo entered the shop before I decided to walk across the street. I glanced in the display window at the rudimentary shelving of cheese wheels and what looked like plastic *baguettes* in the window.

Clearly, the cheese seller had gone to no great trouble to create a display of an outdoor picnic featuring a wine bottle already opened and enjoyed—presumably by the cheese seller himself—along with a couple of desiccated apples.

I didn't blame the proprietor for not going to much trouble to lure people into his shop with a captivating window display. After all, this was France. He could've parked his garbage bins in the window and the customers would still come in to buy cheese.

Through the window I saw Matteo's shadow as he moved through the interior of the shop. On impulse I walked to the door, looked over my shoulder to see if anyone was watching, and then eased it open and crept inside.

8

The old wooden floors creaked under my shoes as I entered the shop. The display window on the front wall admitted a perfect rectangle of sunlight that illuminated fine dust motes drifting through the air. Elsewhere in the shop, tall shelving stretched from floor to ceiling and were loaded with rounds of cheese in various sizes—some pristinely wrapped, others developing bloomy rinds of mold.

I stepped soundlessly toward the center of the shop, the sides of which were lined with wide shelves holding stacked jars of local honey, jam preserves and dried herbs harvested from the hillsides. I scanned the surroundings for any clues, however subtle, that might shed light on the cheese seller's disappearance.

The first thing I noticed was that the shelves had obviously been disturbed. Various sized wheels of cheese and stacks of jars were all sitting at odd angles, as if knocked around in a scuffle. A jar of fig preserves sat shattered on the floor and hadn't been cleaned up. Scuff marks seemed to lead to the back door. Toward the back of the shop, a high counter displayed sample wedges and cheese cubes for customers to try.

"What are you doing here?" Matteo said loudly, startling me as I stood there scanning the shop's shelves.

I hadn't seen him crouching behind the counter.

"Omigosh, you scared me," I said.

"You shouldn't be here," he said crossly.

Detective Sergeant Matteo carried himself with an air of assurance that bordered on arrogance. In his thirties, he wasn't bad looking. He was clearly vain about his hair which was always impeccably styled, and his uniform was always pressed and tidy.

"Why? Is it a crime scene?" I asked.

"No. Nobody's saying that."

Matteo was proud of his ability to keep what he knew to himself—which was ironic since he was usually quite bad at it.

"So what's going on? Where's the cheese seller?" I asked. "I just came from the *boulangerie* and people there are saying nobody has seen him for two days."

"What people?" Matteo asked narrowing his eyes at me.

I realized he himself must have been flapping his gums around town saying things he shouldn't and was worried it was coming back to bite him on the *derriere*.

"Oh, you know, just people," I said evasively. "So, what's the deal? Do you have any leads?"

"Shouldn't you be home baking a pie or something?"

"Ha ha. Very funny."

I have to say that Matteo and I have a very strange history. Now that I think about it, I suppose that's true of just about every person I know in Chabanel but with him it's even truer. I sort of hate him and I wouldn't be surprised if he feels the same about me but there were a couple of incidents over the years that at least on the surface seemed to fly in the face of that.

For example, he once agreed to marry me in order to keep me from ending up in a concentration camp that the French government had set up for all the expats and aliens left displaced by the EMP. He'd also once risked his life to save mine.

Before and after both of these events, we continued to bicker like two siblings locked in a lifelong grudge match. I hate to say it, but I fear—and I don't use that word lightly in reference to Matteo—that deep, deep down there is probably a serious reservoir of affection and respect between us.

Ugh. Now putting the cap on *that* particularly weird and at this moment not at all helpful pathology, I should also say that Matteo has arrested me no fewer than four times. And I've tried to get him fired twice. So, yeah. We're close.

"I want to help," I said.

"You can do that by letting yourself out," he said, but I could see he was looking where I was now looking—at the scuffed marks on the floor.

"Looks like signs of a struggle," I said.

Matteo frowned and looked at the cheese wheels scattered across the floor.

"Have you checked the register?" I asked.

"I was just about to," he said.

He turned and pulled out a cash box from a shelf under the counter. He was wearing gloves—which I was heartened to see—and he opened the box using two fingers of his gloved hand.

"Empty," he said.

"Interesting," I said. "So this is either a theft which would be weird since why would a thief then take the shop owner? Or Monsieur Montrachet left in a hurry and took traveling money with him."

"There is a third possibility," Matteo said as he walked to the back of the store.

I followed him and saw that he'd finally noticed that the scuff marks led to the back door.

"He was dragged away," I said.

"Looks like it." He glanced at me as if suddenly realizing I was still there. "You shouldn't be here."

I knew Matteo was going to use everything that happened between us here to make himself look better to his boss—Luc. I came within a hair's breadth of asking him not to mention to Luc that I'd been here. It annoyed me that I had to think like that. Why was I keeping secrets from Luc? If Matteo didn't want Luc to know—and it would make sense that he wouldn't—that was one thing. But asking him to keep quiet for my sake only amplified the fact that Luc and I were not on the same page. I held up my hands—I was still holding the three baguettes—as if to indicate to Matteo that I gave up and would leave peacefully. I turned to let myself out of the store, still visually sweeping the area for any clues I'd missed.

"If he was abducted," I said over my shoulder, "and there's no ransom note, he's probably dead."

Matteo walked behind me, presumably to lock the door after I left.

"But then why not just kill him in the shop?" he asked. "Why take him?"

"Maybe they wanted to buy themselves time," I said as I stood with my hand on the doorknob to the front door.

"Time for what?"

"Guess you'll find that out when you catch the guy."

"It won't be a ransom," he said, shaking his head. "Montrachet has no family."

"None at all?"

"None that I've ever heard of."

"Be rough for the village to get along without a cheese seller," I commented.

"You're not suggesting the kidnapper will demand ransom from the village?" he asked with a laugh.

"Sounds stupid when you put it like that."

Except this was France. No village can live without cheese for long. Even in the worst of the apocalypse, cheese was the first thing—even before wine—that the black market made easily available.

"I wouldn't mention this to your husband," he said as he leaned past me to open the door to let me out.

"I'm way ahead of you," I said.

As I exited the shop, my mind still on where the cheese seller might be and why I was so uncomfortable being honest with Luc, I saw a movement in my periphery that caught my attention. On the corner of the street, an older gentleman was standing in the shadow of a doorway, peeking at me and apparently thinking himself hidden.

Even at a distance, I could see there was something odd about him loitering in the shadows. The way he seemed to be deliberately straining to observe the front of the cheese shop without being seen set my detective's senses tingling.

As soon as he noticed me looking at him, he abruptly turned to walk down the street away from me. As I watched him go, I wondered what he was doing here. He didn't look like a thief or a stalker. Was he someone who knew the cheese shopkeeper? If so, did he know where he was?

Was he the kidnapper?

Or worse?

9

That evening the temperatures had cooled. From where I knelt in front of the stove, I could see through the open front door where the shadows lengthened across the lawn in front of the cottage. I turned and peered into the stove interior. Luc had gotten word to me that he was too busy to pick up dinner, so I'd done it. The chicken I'd gotten in the village sat in the pan in the oven, but nothing was happening. It looked just as pale and anemic as when I'd seasoned it and slid it into the oven. I stood up and went to look in the firebox. Right away I saw that the fire I thought I'd started hadn't caught.

Cursing to myself, I quickly crumpled more newspaper to stuff into the firebox and topped it with kindling. I lit a match and blew on the tiny flame as soon as it caught the paper. As the kindling began to crackle and pop, I placed a small log on top of it all. You'd think after three years of having to rely on fires to cook and wash I'd be proficient at starting one, but it still takes me just as much time as it did in the beginning. I pulled up a chair to watch the smoke swirl and billow from the grate on the top of the stove.

At this rate it was going to take all night to get the thing hot enough to actually roast a chicken. I felt a wave of discouragement. Nothing seemed to be working in my life at the moment.

I'd had all afternoon to think about what I'd learned today with Matteo at the cheese shop, but I kept coming back to the confounding belief that I wasn't sure what to make of anything—particularly the part where Luc blew me off by saying the case was well in hand only to find out otherwise. Not only was the case *not* well in hand but it was obvious from my walk through Hèlo's cheese shop that we were looking at an abduction.

So why did Luc tell me it was sorted?

I got up to shove another piece of wood into the firebox since the fire seemed to have finally gotten going. I knew that once Matteo told Luc what he'd deduced from the cheese shop, the case would take on a whole different tenor —one that Luc would then be inclined to treat as a serious crime. I didn't expect that to alter anything as far as he and I were concerned—although it seriously disappointed me that Luc didn't want to use my brain for help in any way.

I glanced out the door again to the front yard. I'd been anxiously waiting for Luc to get home all afternoon. But when he did, he immediately changed out of his work clothes into his yard clothes and went to chop wood for our endless need of it for hot water for washing, cooking and warmth. The bulk of the winter was behind us, thank goodness, and before that I'd been living with the twins. In fact, it wasn't until I married Luc this spring that I saw how truly primitively he lived.

Not only did *La Fleurette* have everything all set up for life-after-the-apocalypse, but frankly the twins did most of the work. I'd offered to help but they were the ones with all the necessary knowledge and skills—sewing, planting, food prepping, cooking and baking. My own schooling had been woefully lacking in that regard. In my defense, I had logically assumed that a Liberal Arts education was all I needed to get through a life that offered automatic dishwashers and online banking. I hadn't counted on an apocalypse stranding me in a village in a remote part of France.

Mind you, when I lived with them, I still chopped wood, lugged endless buckets of water up and down hills, and did all the necessary donkeywork to keep the garden alive and weeded as well as tending to our livestock, not to mention dealing with the various shady characters that kept the three of us stocked in coffee beans, chocolate and wine.

I held my hand to the stove and was relieved to feel the heat.

But it seemed, as Luc's wife, I was required to do it all. All except for the black market stuff. It appeared that my engagement with the black market was considered unseemly for a police chief's wife. As a result, I was still working on finding our coffee and chocolate through legitimate avenues. So far, no luck.

"Everything all right, *chérie*?" Luc called from the open door.

"Perfect!" I called back as I used a spatula to push a few more sticks around the firebox to get them animated.

Luc was probably expecting to detect the aromas of his cooking dinner by now. And if I hadn't stupidly let the fire go out, he would've. My shoulders sagged in discouragement. I wasn't sure if I should drag the roasting pan out of the oven while I waited for the oven to get hot or if I should just leave it there.

Deciding to leave it, I turned back to the counter where a mound of half-chopped vegetables littered the cutting board. I looked at the various spices that I'd brought over from *La Fleurette* since I still don't have a working *potager* and tried to remember if I'd seasoned the chicken before I'd put it in the pan.

Whoever said cooking is therapeutic? I wondered in bewilderment. I got an image of Justine and Lèa both going about the kitchen at *La Fleurette* stirring, sifting, chopping, kneading, and Justine at least always had a smile on her face. Few things could prompt that miracle in Lèa, so I didn't fault kitchen prep work for not prompting it.

Cooking dinner for Luc tonight was a big deal for me. It was a big deal because I don't feel confident cooking. Beyond following basic recipes, I really have little interest in learning either. But food was a love language that I knew Luc spoke. Me, doing this for him—and the effort it was taking!—would tell him more than words could how much I wanted to please him. But I worried that my efforts would only encourage him to want this kind of effort nightly. And that, I was not signing up for.

I went back to check the firebox again and was relieved to see that it was going strong. Even so, dinner was going to be much later than even the French liked to eat by the time I got everything on the table. I grabbed a pot and filled it with the water I'd brought in from the outdoor well and set it on one of the burners. It wasn't hot enough to get anything boiling but that was just as well since the chicken was still raw.

Why had I not thought about all of this when I told Luc I'd be happy to move into his place? Had I even known what I was in for? Right up until the wedding, we'd planned that he'd move into *La Fleurette* with me and the twins. I wasn't sure what had changed or at what point I'd agreed to come to his place instead. Maybe I hadn't wanted the twins to end up being his cooks and housekeepers which they surely would've been if we'd stayed. I glanced out the window and saw Luc still chopping wood. His muscles flexed rhythmically as he swung the axe with practiced precision, each forceful strike biting into the wood, sending chips flying while the pile of neatly split logs on the ground grew.

I was probably so keen on making my new husband happy that I just agreed to it without really thinking about what I was agreeing to. I wiped my brow. I knew my hair was hanging limp in messy tendrils escaping its pins. I looked around the kitchen. All the countertops were full of items: a cutting board, a pile of knives, a bowl of flour. There was even a big wooden spoon on the floor. The sink of course was full of dirty dishes and pans.

The whole scene looked like a culinary crime scene, with me its frazzled perpetrator.

Luc came in then and seemed to be seeing the same scene of culinary destruction that I was. I forced myself to smile.

"Dinner is going to be a little late tonight," I said.

To his credit, he simply shrugged.

"Time for a bath then," he said.

I nodded and glanced at the stove, but he waved away my concern.

"I'll put a metal bucket on the fire outside," he said.

"You have a fire going outside?"

"Just a small one."

The very thought of being able to take a hot bath filled me with a sudden longing.

"Sure, plenty of time for a bath," I said cheerfully. "Care for company?"

He laughed and came over to give me a kiss before turning back for the door.

"It looks like you have your hands full getting dinner on the table," he said.

I didn't take the rejection personally. Well, not too personally. I understood that to a Frenchman, the choice between a dinner or a bath with his wife was about on the same level of preference. Let's just say that I knew this in my head. But in my heart, I found it hard to believe. Nonetheless, I kept the smile on my face as he left, and then turned back to the stupid stove with the stupid uncooked chicken in it.

Two hours later, Luc was out of his bath and dinner was on the table. And what a sorry table it was. The chicken sat congealed in its juices, pale and clearly undercooked. Next to it was the charred remains of a loaf of bread I'd gotten from the *boulangerie* and limp, gray-green vegetables that I'd plainly overcooked. A musty spoiled odor wafted in the air nearly blotting out the scent of the charred bread.

"Jules," Luc said with frustration as he surveyed the table setting from his chair. "This is inedible."

"Don't sugar coat it, Luc," I said crossly. "I only spent the whole afternoon creating it."

"That makes it even worse," he said as he ran a hand through his hair. He looked around the kitchen. "Is there nothing else to eat?"

"Look, Luc," I said, tossing down my dinner napkin, "I'm not a cook, okay?"

"No, Jules," he said, his face reddening with his burgeoning annoyance probably made worse by hunger pains. "It's *not* okay. What if I were to say 'sorry, I can't do my job. Too bad?'"

"Are you serious?" I asked. I gestured to the table. "This isn't my job."

"Well, whose it?" he asked.

"Seriously?" I suddenly found it difficult to breathe.

"Why do you keep saying that?" he said, standing up and scraping his chair back under the table.

"Because I can't believe you're really saying this," I said loudly. "Because I keep thinking you must be joking!"

"Why would I joke about not having dinner?" he asked, his voice raised now too. "Do you know how many people at work ask me if I'm eating enough?"

"What does that have to do with me?"

"Can you really ask me that question?" he asked, scratching his head in the very picture of bewilderment. He looked again at the table. "This is...*unsupportable*!"

"You took the words right out of my mouth!" I shouted at him as he turned his back on me to dig out his mobile phone. I knew that could only mean he was getting an emergency phone call.

"Yes?" he said, answering the phone.

He listened for a moment and then looked at me. I don't know how, in that brief glance exchange, I knew his phone call had to do with the missing cheese seller. Maybe because Matteo and I had figured out that foul play was involved and honestly, the two of us were both just waiting for the other shoe to drop.

"Where?" he asked.

"What is it?" I asked. "Is it the cheese seller? Is he found?"

"I'll be right there," Luc said before disconnecting.

"It's the cheese seller, isn't it?" I asked.

"I need to go," Luc said as he patted his trousers for his car keys. "Don't wait up."

"You can't even tell me if it's him?" I asked in frustration.

"Yes!" he said, whirling around on me. "Yes, it's him. Dead. Satisfied?"

I think by the look on his face he knew he'd gone too far with that last retort, but I also know that Luc is the kind of man that once he digs himself in deep, he's going to be clueless as to how to dig himself out again. He gave me an ashamed look and turned and bolted for the door.

And honestly? Since I had my hand on the bowl of undercooked carrots, it was probably not a minute too soon.

10

A cold, misty rain had fallen over the darkened field where Luc stood. It was a stretch of flat, open ground carpeted with muddy grass with wisps of fog drifting between the tree silhouettes in the distance. He was careful to pick his way around the irregular patches of wet ground, hearing as he did the telltale squelch of disturbed earth.

He could see trampled vegetation and disturbed rock crumbles by the beam of his flashlight, whether from the crime scene or the two officers processing it, it was hard to say. The soil was dense, with clumps of moist clay and silty sediment that had been deposited during previous flooding of the area.

The field was about a half mile from the village. It wasn't one that locals spent much time in because of its boggy nature. The owner had left the area when the EMP first hit. It hadn't been sold to anyone and because of its marshy attributes, it was never planted. Even livestock found the grass watery and devoid of nutrients. Luc looked around the dark field and thought it a strange place to dump a body.

Matteo had set up a perimeter around where the body was found by a couple traveling on the d'Eguilles road a hundred feet away. They said their dog had gotten away from them and when they went to recapture her, they found her digging up a human hand in the marsh.

Matteo trudged over to him.

"You got a camera?" Luc asked.

"Serge is bringing one," Matteo responded. "It's definitely Montrachet though. I recognize him."

"Any obvious signs of how he died?"

Luc stood at the perimeter of the cordon for a moment and then slipped under it. The air was thick with the metallic tang of blood mingling with the earthy scent of the early morning dampness as Luc took in the grim tableau before him. The victim's unseeing eyes stared blankly at the gradually lightening sky above. A harsh, crimson slash across the throat marred the placid expression on the man. The ground beneath his head was dark with blood, the surrounding grass lay flattened and boggy.

"Garroted," Matteo said.

Luc winced at Matteo's word. *Garroted*. That was unusual. Most farmers around here had rifles for varmint control. Domestic disputes that ended in homicide were usually strangulation or blunt force trauma.

"The ME said two hours was the soonest he could get here," Matteo said. "And his report a day after that."

Luc nodded. That wasn't unusual. Everything had changed since the EMP had exploded over the Mediterranean three years ago. The whole world had been reset. He looked around the pasture. Was he killed here? Or just dumped here?

"There's something I wanted to show you," Matteo said. "On the body."

Luc squatted next to the body, careful not to touch the ground or it. Matteo reached out to the man's fist and gently uncurled his fingers.

"What is it?" Luc asked.

It was a small gold band with four diamond chips set in it. Luc stared at the ring for a moment before rocking back on his heels. What did this mean? Did the victim snatch the ring off his killer? Did he have it when he left the cheese shop?

"Bag it," he said. "We'll dust it for prints."

"What do you think it means? Crime of passion?"

Luc looked around the field. The road was a good distance from here. If Montrachet had been forced to walk to this spot—but how? at gunpoint?—the killer might possibly be a woman. But if he'd been killed elsewhere? He shook his head. There were too many moving parts right now. He'd think about it later when he had the ME's preliminary report.

"We can't leave him here," Luc said with a frown.

It was bad enough that he could already see signs that animals had been nibbling on the body.

"I can set up a guard," Matteo suggested.

"You volunteering?"

Matteo sighed. "If you need me to."

"Never mind," Luc said. "I'll do it."

He might as well. After the fight he'd had with Jules there was no point in going home. His stomach growled.

"Your bride not feeding you, sir?" Matteo said with a grin.

Luc knew he should laugh but it was too close to home. The harsh words he'd exchanged with Jules tonight seemed to reverberate inside his skull. Suddenly Matteo shot out a hand and grabbed Luc's arm.

"Watch out!" Matteo said sharply. "The body, sir!"

Luc looked down stupidly to see he'd stepped on the hand of the body. Somewhere in the back of his mind he'd thought it was a downed tree limb. He flushed with embarrassment and fury and stepped back.

"I'm pretty sure you don't need to tell me how to handle myself at a crime scene," Luc said tightly.

His words rang in his head as the silence grew between them. It didn't matter. Matteo's response was unspoken but loud and clear.

Clearly someone does.

"I don't mind staying," Matteo said again.

"Fine," Luc said, turning away, disgusted and furious with himself but unable to acknowledge his error to his subordinate.

He walked to the other side of the cordoned area, using his flashlight to examine the ground for footprints or tire marks. The area was so boggy that any footprints would've sunk and dissipated within hours. Expecting a footprint at the time of the murder was folly. But still, Luc did it. He did it until he saw Matteo take up his post by the cordoned area to wait for the ME and then Luc went back to his car. He got in and stared at the light that Matteo had put in the ground by the body. Luc's eyes scanned the area, especially to where the body was within the marked-off cordon, its flags fluttering in the light breeze, but his mind was two kilometers away, back at his cottage where Jules probably already lay sleeping, oblivious to his pain, his turmoil. He started the car and began to drive to the village, grinding his teeth in mounting anger.

I'm screwing up. I should've asked Matteo if he searched for the knife or wire. Or if he found Montrachet's wallet.

His mind buzzed annoyingly, and he felt his forehead

become damp. Where was the couple who'd found the body? Had Matteo interviewed them? How much damage had the dog done to the body before they stopped him?

These were all questions he should've asked Matteo before he left.

What is wrong with me?

The night was calm but cloudy, and a light breeze rustled through the grass on both sides of the road as he drove. No stars or moon shone through the dense clouds to illuminate the road ahead. Only the faint glow of his car's headlights disturbed the darkness.

She's made me less good at my job.

He felt a flurry of emotions, mostly anger, as he processed how irrational *that* thought was. How beneath him.

But still. Irrational or not, it was there.

11

Luc drove from the crime scene to the station, his mind buzzing unpleasantly the entire time but unfortunately not due to theories or observations about his murder case. He pulled up to the front of the Chabanel police station and sat for a moment while the engine of his Citroen clicked and shuddered after he turned it off. Madame Gabin wasn't due in for at least another two hours. He rubbed a hand over his face and tried to bring to mind the image he'd seen an hour earlier—Hèlo Montrachet's body spread eagled in a field, clearly the victim of a deadly assault—and then winced because all he could seem to think about was the argument he'd had with Jules just before the call had come in.

Frustration boiled up inside him as he got out of the car, slamming the door and hearing it echo through the quiet village streets as he tried to push thoughts of her out of his mind.

By the time he'd unlocked the station door and let himself in, the weariness of the early hour combined with the stress of the ugly words he'd exchanged with Jules had settled firmly, painfully in his gut. He shed his coat on the chair in his office, and sank into his desk chair, rubbing his palms over his face.

So now it was a murder case. Up to now, he'd been hoping Montrachet was off visiting relatives or absent in some way that his disappearance was easily explained. He shook his head in self-disgust. Matteo's report yesterday had made an easy answer to Montrachet's disappearance increasingly unlikely. Was there something Luc should have done between learning that a scuffle had occurred in the cheese shop and finding the man's body in a field with his throat cut?

He stood up, restless in spite of his weariness, his quarrel with Jules playing in an irritating, endless loop in his mind. Frustration mounted inside him like a pressure about to burst. With a guttural sound of vexation, he slammed a fist onto his desk, making papers and file folders jump at the impact.

With a steadying breath, he turned and went to the staff room to brew a pot of strong coffee, hoping that might jolt his flagging spirit back to some vestige of productivity. Or at least help snap his mind back to work. But as soon as he poured the water over the coffee grounds he found himself staring at the pot of slowly perking coffee and all he felt was the weariness of a brain battered by stresses beyond his control.

He watched the steady, monotonous drip-drip-drip of the coffee as it filled the pot, focusing on it like a Zen master trying to distract himself from the buzzing discord that was filling his brain and slowly driving him mad.

∽

The village square was usually a place of quaint charm and communal laughter, although at the moment it felt like an amphitheater of dark judgment to the killer who crouched in a thick rosemary bush.

The weight of the deed committed was like a relentless, suffocating force that seemed to grow with every beat of a guilty heart.

Why should I feel guilty? Hèlo deserved to die! I'm just sorry I couldn't kill him twice!

A tremor in the hands led to a need to rub them together which prompted an image of a diabolical cartoon villain which then triggered an irrational urge to laugh which had to be quickly quelled. Deserving or not, Chief DeBray would surely not see any of this as amusing.

Repositioning the branches helped ease the ache in cramping muscles from sitting in the bushes for so long. But had coming here and taking up this ridiculous sentry position really been necessary? Yes, it had. Of course it had. Amazingly, no sooner had the belief began to form that it had been a fool's errand to crouch hidden in a rosemary bush in the wee hours of the morning, when none other than the chief of Chabanel police had driven past.

So they've discovered the body. That was fast.

The chief got out of his car looking very much like the weight of the world was on his shoulders. Perhaps it might also be his new marriage? Everyone knew the American was a handful—and not in a good way. Or was it because, deep down—gruesome crime scene or not—even the chief knew that Hèlo was better off dead? The whole village was better off with Hèlo dead. The whole of Provence—of France!—was better off.

Suddenly, in spite of these encouraging thoughts, a

kernel of guilt developed deep inside that all the swallowing could not dispel. The killer's head bowed as if in penance.

It is indefensible what I did. I know that. A part of me is disgusted by it—like any good person would be. But it had to be done. And who else could do it but me? It was a terrible act necessary to protect a greater good.

The chief went inside the police station. The killer was sure there had been no evidence to find except that which had been deliberately left. It was a shame not to watch the police as they processed the scene. But that was too dangerous to have arranged. It wouldn't be much of a triumph if a life's sentence in prison was the consequence for having done everyone such an immense favor.

The light in the front room of the police station clicked on and the killer watched Chief DeBray walk to the back room.

Probably to put the coffee pot on.

A smile edged around bloodless lips.

Like that will make any difference in the end.

12

The next morning, I opened my eyes and saw the morning light filtering in through a hazy blanket of cloud cover from my bedroom window. Despite the humidity that I could already feel on my skin even from inside the bedroom, the sunlight seemed to give the day's start a dreamlike feeling.

Summer in Provence was hot. It wasn't terrible yet, but it would get there.

I lay in bed gazing out the window and trying not to think. Luc had not come home last night which I thought mildly surprising since any job that required working all night—unless he was interviewing a suspect—should have been delegated to someone of lower rank.

On the other hand, I didn't blame him for wanting to be any place but home. I don't know how things got so out of control. One minute we were both just simmering with resentment and the next we were screaming at each other. Maybe it was just me doing the screaming. Probably Luc was still simmering. He certainly wasn't talking.

It occurred to me that I might mention to him how

important communication is in a marriage but after some of the things I said to him last night I wouldn't blame him for not thinking too highly of communication.

I swung my legs out of bed and my bare feet touched the smooth wooden floor. I knew before I even started looking for my clothes that breakfast was going to be too much trouble especially since it involved getting the stupid stove working again. I opted instead for cold *brioche* that I'd gotten from the *boulangerie* a couple of days ago. It was stale but better than nothing. What *wasn't* better than nothing was no coffee. I thought about running over to *La Fleurette* since I knew the twins would have a large jug of French pressed coffee sitting hot on the breakfast table. But if I did that, they'd wonder why I didn't just make my own coffee at home.

Justine was more forgiving than Lèa when it came to what they both considered my inherent laziness, but even Justine would raise an eyebrow if I were to come over to get coffee instead of making it at home two days in a row. Both twins were committed to seeing me happily married. They were also both firmly in Luc's camp and had been since the beginning. And why wouldn't they be? Luc was a great guy. Loyal, brave, logical, sexy as hell. Check, check, check and check.

As I ate my stale *brioche* and washed it down with well water that tasted vaguely of cow manure, I pulled on cotton slacks and a pullover sweater and thought of the job ahead of me today. I work as a private investigator—although that definition is very stretchy since the EMP. To that end, I've done everything from surveillance to actual skip tracing—non-electronically, of course. I wish there were more cases for me to investigate around here but I tend to get most of my money—and by money, I mean produce or milk or wine

—from cases that involve me sitting in a tree waiting for one of my client's spouses to do something they shouldn't.

I've been stoned (not the fun kind) and shot at and everything in between and somehow, I'm still doing it. Maybe that's because even after three years of living here, my French is still at the second-grade level which seriously restricts my options. I know I should work on my language skills, but I'm managing well enough so there's a definite lack of motivation.

I looked around the kitchen and saw the dishes from last night still congealing on the counter. I would've washed them but that required hot water and if I'm not bothering with a fire to make coffee, I'm certainly not bothering with a fire to wash dishes. I had a shimmer of guilt at the thought of Luc coming home today and seeing the dishes still not done, and immediately felt a flash of anger.

If he doesn't like it, he can wash them!

I stood and brushed the *brioche* crumbs from my sweater to the floor. If I had my dog with me, she'd have made short work of the crumbs. Cocoa is a medium-sized shepherd mix who saved my life a couple of years ago and who I love like my own child. Luc was fine with my bringing her with me to live here but his lukewarm acquiescence combined with the looks on Justine and Lèa's face when I suggested taking her made me reconsider.

I go to *La Fleurette* at least once a day so it's not like I don't see her, but I'm used to sleeping with her. And feeding her and playing with her and brushing her. Honestly, there's something about taking care of an animal that's soothing to both you and it. When I was a teenager back in Atlanta, I was into horseback riding. I used to spend the same amount of time at the barn grooming my horse as I did riding him. I miss running my fingers through Cocoa's fur. I think it helps calm me. In any case, I don't have her here so before I go down that road of reflecting on all the things I no longer have, I need to decide if I was really missing my dog or if I was just intent on building a ledger of wrongs to set before my new husband.

I stepped outside the cottage and instantly saw the plot of ground that Luc and I had decided would be the kitchen *potager*. It was still just a clump of dirt. I closed the garden gate behind me—carefully keeping in heaven knows what since we have no livestock or chickens—or children for that matter.

As I walked down the path to the driveway where my bike was propped up against an ancient plane tree, I found myself very aware of the fact that I'd been consciously keeping my meeting this morning a secret. I don't consider it a lie not to have mentioned it to Luc. If anything, I'm doing him a favor. I know he doesn't love what I'm still doing for a living so, in the spirit of trying to keep things light between us, I made a conscious point not to mention it.

Naturally, when I thought about it, that bothered me, but I decided not to dwell on it.

~

Luc was awakened from where he'd fallen asleep, his head on his desk, an undrunk mug of cold coffee by his hand and the aroma of freshly baked rolls and rich coffee swirling around his office. He lifted his head as Madame Gabin entered the room, carrying a tray with steaming mugs.

"You look terrible," she said.

Luc's stomach grumbled in response, reminding him that he hadn't eaten since lunch the day before. He stood up and glanced at the clock. He'd slept four hours. Matteo must still be at the crime scene. He felt a flush of self-disgust. All he'd done was come to the office to sleep on his desk while Matteo spent the night in the pasture waiting for the medical examiner.

"Are you leaving?" Madame Gabin asked him with surprise.

"There's been a murder," he said. "I'll take one of those for Matteo." He took both cups of coffee from her.

"Where is he?" Madame Gabin asked.

"Sitting in a field waiting for the ME from Aix to show up," Luc said as he picked up a *pain au chocolat* that was on the tray and took a large bite, registering his sharp hunger and also Madame Gabin's look of surprise when he did. He picked up another pastry and then turned toward the door, still not quite alert from his brief nap on the desktop.

"I can have Serge run the coffee out to him," Madame Gabin protested. "You shouldn't be doing that. Why don't you head home for a proper meal?"

Luc began to laugh and by the time he stopped, he could see that Madame Gabin was looking at him with an increasingly worried look. He put down one of the coffees.

"Yeah, okay, have Serge deliver the coffee," he said.

"Are you going home?" she asked, her voice laced with concern.

He took a bite of the other *pain au chocolat* and looked at her.

"Have I told you how much I value your contributions, Madame Gabin?" he asked, tilting his head. "You always know just the right thing to say."

"I do?" she asked, now looking more worried than ever.

"But I think a brisk walk and another coffee is what I need at the moment. If the medical examiner or Matteo shows up, have someone come for me at the Café Provençal."

"Of course, Chief," she said, still eyeing him suspiciously.

Luc walked out the front door and gulped down his coffee. The day's sunlight seemed to burn into his eyelids. On the other hand, the coffee was already buzzing through his veins, and he felt more alert.

Focus on the case.

He got an image of the body again, lying in the moonlight in the field. Something was strange about it. Aside from the obvious. Something didn't feel right. Or was it just the never-ending horror of seeing a man alert and alive one minute and moribund and lifeless the next? He never really got used to that. As long as he was in law enforcement, he didn't think he ever would.

He stepped off the curb and headed towards the village center when he heard someone calling his name.

"*Mon cher inspecteur*! Fancy meeting you here."

He looked up to see Mèmè LaDonc grinning at him. Mèmè was relatively new to Chabanel and had created an immediate stir—especially among the Chabanel wives. With dancing brown eyes and a quick laugh, she was a renowned flirt. Jules often teased Luc about how much he enjoyed the attention from Mèmè. He couldn't deny he was flattered by it.

"Ça va *bien*, Mèmè?" Luc replied with his first smile of the day.

She hurried to walk beside him, and he detected a scent of musk and floral notes. He tried to remember the last time Jules had worn perfume.

"Join me for coffee?" Mèmè asked. "You look like you could use some cheering up."

Luc knew immediately that, teasing or not, Jules would not be happy with him having coffee with Mèmè. Just as he was about to shake his head, he found himself craving the easy smile and pleasant acceptance that Mèmè was offering. A meal and a friendly chat would do him good.

"I *could* use some cheering up," he said.

"Don't tell me your new bride is not taking care of you?" Mèmè said with a giggle as she took his arm.

He smiled at her and felt the ponderous weight of the morning begin to lift away. Why should he feel guilty about having a coffee with a friend? He wasn't doing anything wrong.

And then when he thought of Jules and her friendship with the historian Davos, it was all he could do not to actually put his arm around Mèmè's shoulder as they walked together toward the café.

13

Katrine had just dropped the girls off at early childcare at Madame Petit's when she glimpsed Luc and that LaDonc woman walking arm in arm toward the Provençal Café.

She literally took a step back in shock when she saw them and then stopped walking altogether so she could better observe the scene before her. Mèmè was leaning in close to Luc, her hand holding his arm as she whispered something in his ear. Luc seemed captivated by whatever she was saying, his eyes sparkling with amusement. Katrine watched them until they disappeared inside the café.

With a feeling of heaviness expanding to her core, Katrine continued past the café on her way to *la Mairie*. If she hadn't seen it with her own eyes, she would not have believed it. Luc DeBray—all of two months married and carrying on with the biggest flirt in the village. There wasn't a wife in Chabanel who didn't have a suspicious eye on Madame LaDonc. Was what Katrine had seen innocent? Luc hadn't looked as if he was attempting to hide his pleasure in Madame LaDonc's company. And, especially on the heels of Jules' comments to Katrine yesterday—about how Luc was perhaps less than happy with her—wasn't this actually something to worry about?

And the biggest question of all: *Should I tell Jules?*

Katrine bit her lip and glanced back toward the café. But if it was nothing, telling Jules would just cause problems that didn't need to happen. Katrine's mind raced with her conflicting thoughts. But by the time she reached the square where *la Mairie* was located, she was already chewing over a whole new set of problems. She had a series of meetings this morning that she wasn't remotely prepared for. The village oversight committee seemed to think she could single handedly bring new business and job opportunities to the village.

In the middle of an apocalypse?

Plus, there had been several matters from her predecessor that needed to be cleaned up and Katrine had no idea how to start on that. She imagined Jules would have no problem bulldozing her way into a situation that she knew she wasn't qualified to handle. That was Jules all over.

The fact was, the more Katrine thought of it, the more she couldn't help but think how everything had always gone Jules's way ever since she showed up in Chabanel. While it was true there had been a few bumps in the road—Jules' near escape of being incarcerated at the alien's detainment camp, the betrayal by Katrine's husband and Jules' eventual marriage to a psychotic serial killer—the fact remained that Jules had wriggled out of every one of those catastrophes no worse for wear. If anything, she'd benefited!

Jules wasn't the one who was left raising two girls on her own while her husband was in prison. Even now, Gaultier wrote Katrine begging for her forgiveness and saying he had changed. What a relief it would be on so many different levels if she could believe him. The divorce had not yet gone through and when it did it would not financially benefit Katrine in any way. Worse, as her mother kept reminding her, she would then have to present herself—at her age—as a divorced woman. Well, of course the existence of her daughters also announced that, but that had much less a stain attached to it.

Gaultier asked for nothing in his weekly letters; just her forgiveness, some photos of her and the girls, and perhaps a few euros to buy cigarettes. The fact was, if not for Jules, Gaultier would be home right now, sharing the hard work of raising two children and trying to make a living. It was true he was lazier than she'd have liked but he was always amenable to doing as she asked. She tried to imagine how much easier her life would be today if she had someone like that to help out! A partner who was willing to do whatever you asked of them!

Katrine went up the flat wide steps of *la Mairie*, the village city hall, suddenly feeling as if a heavy weight had settled on her shoulders. Once inside, she nodded at the receptionist who looked at her with surprise to see her so early. She made her way to her second-floor office and set her battered brief case down on her desk—an antique that had been worn smooth by generations of Chabanel mayors.

From her large multi-paned window, Katrine could take in the whole of the village square below. In the center stood the war memorial—a simple stone obelisk listing the names of all the young Chabanel men who had never returned from battle. From the monument, cobblestone streets radiated out like the spokes of a wheel, each lined with buildings that housed shops and homes. Beyond the monument, stood an army of leafed-out plane trees, aged but dignified, forming a perimeter, as their broad canopies met over the square to offer shade from the hot Provençal sun.

Bells ominously pealed the hour from the opposite end of the square, where the village church was located, their ringing seeming to carry on the breeze far into the countryside. Villagers milling about below, stopping to chat or browse wares from open bins in the various shops made Katrine think that this was a scene that had changed little over the decades, enduring through wars and times of plenty alike. From her high vantage point, she felt connected to the peaceful rhythm of daily village life as it played out serenely below.

Katrine could easily see the red-tiled roof of the café where Luc and Mèmè LaDonc had gone. She felt a flush of resentment ripple through her. Nor did Jules have a difficult mother who spent every waking moment telling her what a disappointment she was or how her husband probably wouldn't have committed his many crimes if she'd been a better wife. It was true that technically none of Katrine's current hardships were Jules's fault. Jules always walked away unscathed from disaster after disaster leaving a trail of broken promises and misunderstandings behind her. It would never occur to Jules that she was responsible for any of it.

Katrine turned away from the window and sat at her desk. She looked at her work diary with its endless list of things to do today. Legislative duties, editing existing regulations, creating new laws to address the ever changing needs of a post-apocalyptic village. She forced herself not to groan out loud as her eyes ran down the list and then looked out the window again. She couldn't help but wonder what Luc was doing with Madame LaDonc at the café right this minute. Luc was such a good man. Was it possible that Jules' high-handed ways had finally succeeded in alienating him? Luc, a man loyal and true, a man that any woman in the village would kill to be with? Maybe the fact of Luc turning to a *Frenchwoman* for comfort and understanding was one of the more believable episodes of his relationship with Jules. Katrine felt a tiny shiver of guilt at the thought.

The warm aroma of freshly brewed coffee wound its way up the stairs to where she sat, reflecting. Her assistant would be up shortly with a cup and probably a nice fresh raison *brioche* too. She eased back in her chair and began to feel the tightly knotted kinks of her thoughts begin to slowly relax.

If Luc really was cheating on Jules that was terrible. Of course, it was. But all things considered, maybe it was understandable too.

Maybe in fact, it was karma.

14

After spending the last two hours talking with a very chatty woman who was only somewhat connected to my investigation of the ongoing dispute between two neighboring farms about a shared pastureland, I was already feeling more than a little wrung out. Even so, the case was an interesting one. It seemed that for generations, there had been an informal agreement between these two families over a twenty-five acre pasture that straddled their adjacent properties. For years, both families let their livestock graze freely on the open field.

Then, out of the blue, one of the families—a Monsieur Girard—decided he wanted to fence off his half and sell the land for development. His neighbor, Monsieur Robert, argued that this would ruin his farming operation. Since then, there had been several unpleasant incidents between the families over access to the disputed pasture. Tensions had only escalated. Both sides accused the other of harassment, vandalism and threats. My interviewee this morning had been hard to keep on point and because I wasn't the police or official in any real capacity, I was more or less forced to go along with her flow.

I'd been hired by Katrine in her capacity as the mayor of Chabanel to investigate the facts behind both families' claims to the land over the decades so that she could make a final determination—to which both families had agreed. It's the *over the decades* part which was key here. In the States, you'd just look at the plat and decide who owned what. But what went before—the history of a place—mattered in France. It mattered as much or more than whatever the plat said.

As a result, I have spent hours poring over historical deeds, surveys, tax records and old maps of the property boundaries. I've conducted interviews with elderly locals, like the woman I'd spoken with this morning, to unearth long-standing land use traditions as well as the history of the properties. Bit by bit a picture was forming. But the best part of that was that I wasn't the one to have to decide what the picture showed. That was Katrine's job.

As I coasted into the gravel drive of *La Fleurette* I heard Cocoa barking from the back garden. She must have heard my bike tires on the pebbles. Two of the twins' three largely feral cats sat cleaning themselves on the front half stone wall of the porch eyeing me suspiciously—although of course I'd lived here with them for three years. Neige—French for *snow*, even though she's black—has been around the longest, and then there's Camille. Tiny Tim was relatively new, a foundling and a bit of an outlier. Kind of like me.

Cocoa's advance warning seemed to trigger the front door being flung open before I'd even finished parking my bike. Justine stood in the doorway, a dishtowel in her hands.

"You are home," she said.

The twins had agreed to a brief interview session today. I knew I'd need to strike while the iron was semi-warm before they changed their minds. The fact is, they couldn't care less about getting national recognition for what they had done during the war. But it was important to me that they get credit. I'm not even sure why. It just is.

I kissed her on the cheek as I passed into the house where I could smell lunch cooking.

"You were talking with Mimi Simon this morning?" Justine asked as she followed me inside.

I was always amazed at how both Justine and Lèa knew so much about what everyone was doing in the village. After three years, I shouldn't be so surprised.

"I was," I said. "She seemed very sweet."

"Appearances can be deceiving," Lèa said as she came into the room, wiping her hands on a hand towel and critically eyeing my outfit, which was a bit mud-spattered from my ride.

Neither twin had been thrilled with how I'd chosen to make my living as a private investigator. In all honesty, they had a bit of a point. There were many more things that could go wrong while working this profession here in the country than if I'd had an office in a major city like Lyon or Aix.

The fact was, performing my job forces me to spend a good deal of time lurking in pastures, bushes and even trees trying to get evidence of adultery, which makes up a major portion of my clientele. That in itself wouldn't be so bad, but this area of Provence is still littered with undiscovered armaments from the last world war. Incredible, but true. Once, while hiding in a ditch with my camera, I found an unexploded bomb that had to be dealt with by a state-run bomb disposal squad from Lyons. Even after seventy years, these finds still happen all over France, so much so that they have a dedicated department just to handle them. Fascinating, yes, but also somewhat terrifying.

"How does the mayor think silly Mimi Simon can help decide the issue between Monsieur Girard and Monsieur Robert?" Lèa asked.

As I stepped into the kitchen, I saw the table was set for three, confirming that they were expecting me for lunch. Tears sprang to my eyes. I'd loved living here with these two women. I loved *them*. I'm not sure how much I'd missed them until just this minute.

"Well," I said, "Mimi knew the previous owners of both properties fifty years ago."

"She couldn't have been sixteen years old," Justine commented.

"True," I said, "but her testimony will be helpful to Katrine's final decision."

"I cannot imagine how," Justine said.

"Why are you still doing this work?" Lèa said, frowning. "It's extremely unfeminine and invasive of our neighbors."

I could've said that scrambling over the French countryside when she was seventeen with a Sten MkII rifle strapped to her back might be considered a tad unfeminine too, but I refrained.

"I think Mimi enjoyed the company today," I said mildly.

"You can tell us all about it over lunch," Justine said, stepping in front of Lèa as if to physically prevent any more questions from that corner. "Go clean up, *chérie*. And then pour yourself a glass of wine."

I went down the hall to wash my hands, glad to walk away from the defense of what I did for a living. The fact was I enjoyed my work. The job I did today felt like I was helping to mend a community. My final report to Katrine would help her make a decision that would settle the truthful ownership question and put an end to the hostile neighbor dispute once and for all.

As I made my way back to the kitchen, Cocoa romping happily at my heels, I couldn't help but think that this kind of investigative research might seem boring to some people, or even unpleasantly contentious, especially when your subjects didn't want to talk, but I loved it. I'm not sure what that says about me, but there you have it.

The bottom line was that it was a paying job and a good use of my skills. A perfect setup, you might say, if it weren't for the fact that I had to hide it from my husband.

15

Is there anything more welcoming than the savory scent of slow-cooked chicken with mushrooms and onions with hints of garlic and thyme? Not to mention the ever-present flavor note of a rich Provençal wine. *Coq au vin* just happens to be a favorite dish of mine. I'm not saying I've only eaten scrambled eggs and stale *baguettes* since I've been married but, yes, that would be accurate.

"It smells amazing," I said as I moved into the kitchen to look over Justine's shoulder at the stove. Seeing the bubbling concoction made me instantly homesick as her homecooked meals—especially this one—had quickly become the very definition of warmth and comfort for me. I don't remember ever eating it before I came to live in France.

"Surely you have made *coq au vin* since you moved out?" Lèa asked with an arched eyebrow.

"Now, Sister," Justine said. "I've been meaning to show Jules how to make it and have just been busy."

"Of course," Lèa said sarcastically. "It's your fault."

Once we took our places at the kitchen table, I felt the last ounce of tension seep out of me. A perfect meal made by people who love you will do that to you. Cocoa and the cats were in their sentinel positions under the table in case some morsel should drop, and I allowed myself to sit back and enjoy a meal as perfect as anything a Michelin starred restaurant could make.

"Speaking of Luc," Lèa said.

"Were we?" I asked as I reached for the fresh *baguette* on the table. I felt my shoulders begin to tighten up once more.

"All is well there?" she asked.

"Of course. Why wouldn't it be?"

"He would prefer you to stop working, you know," Justine said.

I put down my fork and looked at the two of them.

"Has he said something to you?"

The twins shared a look.

"Not in so many words, *chérie*," Justine said.

"Can we talk about something else? Are you guys free after lunch to answer a few questions about the National Order of Merit application? You mentioned last time I was here that you would."

Justine sighed dramatically.

"If we must," she said.

"I still don't see the point," Lèa said with a scowl.

"The point," I said deliberately, "is to give credit where it is due." I held up a hand to stop her rebuttal. "And before you say anything, I know that's not why you did it. You were at war. But it's important to recognize the things people did —people like you—when the sacrifice was so great. A medal is the least of what your country should do for you."

"What will we do with a medal?" Lèa scoffed. "Put it in a scrapbook?"

"It's history, Lèa," I said. "You affected history by what you did in the war. And this will be a tangible recognition of that. I can't explain it any better."

"Are you doing it for yourself, perhaps?" Lèa asked, narrowing her eyes at me.

I blinked. I'm not blood related to either of them of course. I've only known them for the three years I've been stranded in France. But I love them. If I had kids, I would teach them to love them as their true and absolute grandmothers. And yes, I would show my children the medals and tell their stories over and over again.

"Maybe I am," I said.

Lèa sighed and spooned up the chicken stew onto her plate.

"Yes, well, fine," she said. "In that case."

It was so like them to do it for me when they wouldn't bother doing it for themselves. They truly are the Greatest Generation.

"Oh," I said, "speaking of the Order of Merit project, I got a letter from Davos Bellinort. He's coming back to Chabanel in a few days and I was hoping he could stay at *La Fleurette*."

"We are not answering any of his prying questions," Lèa said.

"You've already made that clear," I assured her.

The fact was, Davos was basically a genius at what he did, which was bringing from the shadows every possible story of the triumph of good over evil during France's darkest hour. And he does it with empathy, humor and respect. I think there is a need for more people who can do that.

"Then why is he coming back?" Justine asked.

"It seems that there's a guy in Aix he's hoping to interview," I said.

"But why is he coming to Chabanel?" Lèa asked.

"To see me," I said in mild exasperation. "Is that okay? You knew we'd become friends."

"Married women don't have men friends," Lèa said.

"How very eighteen hundreds of you."

After that we finished our lunch in relative peace. I did sneak a few crumbs to Cocoa although it certainly appeared as if somebody had been steadily sneaking her table scraps in my absence. After lunch, I washed the dishes while the sisters picked up their knitting and went into the sitting room to wait for me.

I already knew the barebones of what they had done during the war. They were in their teens and worked with the French Resistance in this area. Basically, the Resistance fighters here in Provence, like in the rest of France, were a small, tight-knit group of locals determined to undermine the German occupation. While both twins were detained and questioned at one time or another, neither was sent away to camps, probably because they were young and affected innocence or ignorance. In any case, for years they wouldn't even discuss the war with me or talk about what they'd done during the war.

I knew from my conversations with Davos that the process of gathering intelligence—which was largely what the sisters did during the war—without being detected by German patrols or spies hiding in the local population was particularly dangerous.

Communicating plans within the various resistance groups in France was something else the twins specialized in and was especially hair-raising with the Germans constantly working to intercept messages or discover secret meeting places. One compromised Resistance member could easily mean capture for all. On top of that, there were the physical demands of carrying out the various acts of sabotage under pressure, feats like remaining hidden while slashing tires in the dark or planting explosive devices without being discovered—or accidentally blowing themselves up.

Plus, the sisters and their *copains* had to deal with unpredictable conditions like darkness, cold, rain or any other obstacle that might slow them down or reveal their positions. The psychological strain of living a double life in an occupied community while dodging enemy spies and informants was relentless and harrowing and certainly not for everyone. I'd read some of the first-hand accounts that Davos had gathered which were enough to give you sleepless nights if not absolute nightmares. It's a wonder people did it—the risks were so great. But they did, over and over again.

Lèa and Justine had told me a few stories of fellow Resistance members who'd broken down under the pressure of it all even *before* the Gestapo got their hands on them. Everything the Resistance members did put them in danger of leaving evidence that could reveal them or their families. Literally, a single mistake could be fatal. And often was.

As I was about to learn in greater detail, sometimes even their victories were.

"Tell me about the gas depot," I said.

This was a well-known story in this area of Provence. I happened to know that the twins had been personally involved in pulling it off. If it wasn't the jewel in my petition to *La Grande Chancellerie* to get them their medals, it was darn close.

"You have heard that story a million times," Lèa said with a snort.

"Everyone has," Justine said.

"Not everyone has heard it from people who were actually there," I pointed out.

"Is that so important?" Justine asked.

"It is, in order to help bring the story alive," I said. "And you're right. I'm sure the committee for the National Order of Merit has heard the story. Which is all the more reason why I need live eyewitnesses to describe what happened."

"It was routine."

"So bore me."

"It annoys me when you attempt to be funny," Lèa said with a cross look.

"Let's just tell it and be done with it," Justine said to her sister.

She put her knitting down on the couch beside her and took in a deep breath as if to fortify herself.

"As you know, *chérie*, Lèa and I—and a few others—spent weeks surveilling the depot to learn guard schedules, blind spots, and ways to cut supply lines without harming human life—"

"Not that sparing Nazis was a priority," Lèa pointed out.

"No, but we weren't there to assassinate anyone," Justine said to her sister. "And not all Germans were Nazis."

This was an old debate between the two of them and I didn't want them to get distracted in a side argument.

"You were there to impair German troop movement on the ground," I prompted.

"Yes, and to make it harder for them to attack key allied targets," Lèa said.

"So, your surveillance involved sneaking onto the depot grounds at night to observe their routines, right?" I asked.

"Yes," Justine said. "By the time it came to blowing things up, we knew the depot better than we knew our own village. Are you sure you want to hear all this?"

"Yes, please," I said, as I poised my pencil over my notebook.

"Well, some part of our team was tasked with obtaining the explosives without being traced back to us by German forensic investigation."

"Not that they ever bothered with that," Lèa said ominously.

"Yes, yes," I said. "But *your* roles, specifically?"

Justine straightened out the creases in the long *tablier* over her day dress. Her hands were wrinkled and old but they didn't shake. Not even at her age, not even after everything she'd had to do to get to this age.

"We knew we needed to strike when security was lowest," she said. "That meant at night."

"First, we snuck onto the property," Lèa said, picking up the story, "and drained the fuel tanks of all the jeeps and trucks."

I'd never heard this part before.

"Then we slashed their tires," Lèa said.

"Another part of our group planted the explosives in key areas of the depot," Justine said.

"The explosives part of it wasn't you?" I asked.

Both twins shook their heads but now they weren't looking at me.

"How long did all this take?" I asked.

"Perhaps an hour?" Justine said.

"And nobody saw you this whole time?"

Lèa snorted again.

"Their sentries were asleep. They did not expect defiance from the village sheep."

"We hid in the surrounding woods and detonated the explosives from there," Justine said quietly.

Both twins were silent for a moment. I could see they were reliving that moment when the depot went up like a volcano's fierce awakening, spewing fire and smoke into the night sky. Or maybe they were thinking of what came afterward. I knew from what I'd read—and from what Davos had told me—that the raid itself was considered a minor one but at least for a few hours it was a morale-boosting victory for the Resistance in their struggle to undermine the occupiers.

"I remember how proud of ourselves we were that nobody had died," Justine said softly. "Do you remember, Lèa?'

Lèa nodded grimly. "We thought we were so clever."

The night's damage—at least conceptually—was a source of pride and accomplishment for the Resistance. Unfortunately, the episode resulted in severe consequences. Not only were the Germans able to rebuild the damaged depot fairly quickly, but the next day they went to the nearby village of Sainte-Claire-sur-Mer and selected fifty villagers—men, women and children—who they then dragged to the village square and hung.

I knew both twins found it emotionally devastating to remember what they believed their actions had caused. But I also know that because this particular incident was so horrific and so well documented, it would be singular in the war medals committee's decision to award the twins their medals.

I closed my notebook to signal to them that I wouldn't torture them any more today by making them bring up bad memories. Davos and I had talked about this particular incident at length. Both he and I were sickened by the knowledge that every time the Resistance made any headway in affecting the trajectory of the war in their area, innocent people were made to suffer for their actions.

But then, as anyone will tell you, the Nazis did not play fair.

16

Luc drove home slowly. The rain had held off and the sun had stayed hot all day, so the drive was a steamy one. Even before the EMP, he'd had no air conditioning in his car. The afternoon had been an unproductive one and he didn't feel he'd done much more to move things forward.

His thoughts came back to the memory of Mèmè laughing at just about every word out of his mouth and then putting her hand on his as it rested on the table at the Provencal Café. He'd eaten up the attention like he'd been a schoolboy. What was the matter with him? It was only after they'd parted company—complete with double cheek kisses that he'd never exchanged with her before—that he began to feel truly sickened by his behavior.

The worst of it was when he showed up at the office—hours later in the middle of a murder investigation—to see that Madame Gabin knew exactly where he'd been and with whom. He should've known she'd find out and he burned with shame at the thought. Worse, was the fact that Matteo was waiting for him in the station. Not only had the ME gotten to the crime scene well before expected and finished processing the body in situ, but Matteo had badgered him such that the man had actually delivered a preliminary report on Montrachet's injuries.

Just when Luc was sure he had at least a few hours before he could be expected to start solving the crime—he was already a day behind.

Because he intended to work the evening to make up for his long lunch hour, he decided he'd take Jules into town tonight for an early dinner. They'd both had enough time to cool off. He couldn't even remember now what their argument was about, and he was eager to show her that he was not about to let a little misunderstanding derail them for long. He was in this for the long haul. She needed to know that.

As soon as he stepped into the cottage forecourt, he could tell she wasn't home. Forget the fact that her bike was missing; there was just something vacant and empty about the place. Nonetheless, he opened the front door and stepped inside.

"*Chérie*?" he called. "Are you here?"

Only silence answered him.

He sighed in disappointment and walked into their bedroom where he found the bed made. That was unusual and he felt yet another flinch of guilt ripple through him. While he'd been flirting with Mèmè LaDonc, Jules had been home tidying up their cottage. His stomach turned at the memory of his earlier baser impulses.

Would this be something he and Jules might be able to laugh about later, he wondered?

He looked around the room and felt a spasm of sorrow. His eye landed on the book she was reading by her bedside and impulsively he went to it. He couldn't remember the last time he'd asked her what she was reading or taken an interest in something that was important to her. He picked up the book but before he could glance at the cover, an envelope fell out of it. He stooped to pick it up and realized it was the letter from Davos Bellinort that he'd brought to her yesterday.

He felt a burning sensation in his stomach as he stared at the envelope in his hand. And then he pulled the letter out of the envelope and read it. The letter was mostly about a man in Aix who claimed to have helped escort a dozen or so downed Allied pilots to Spain during the war who Bellinort was clearly excited about interviewing.

"He's ninety-something now so he must have just been a boy during the war," Bellinort wrote. *"It's humbling and amazing to imagine actual children taking these kinds of incredible risks. I can't wait to shake his hand."*

Luc felt his stomach clench at the warm, easy-going style the letter was written in. Not exactly the language of lovers, but certainly the approach of a man comfortable conversing with Luc's wife. Luc felt a flare of jealousy and he swallowed hard as if by doing so he could eradicate it.

It was the last line of the letter that pushed the uncomfortable guilty feeling over the edge into outright anger.

"Can't wait to see you again, Jules. I should be in town the week of the fifth. Until then, mon cher."

At some level Luc knew that if Bellinort had been Jules' brother the signature *mon cher* would have been entirely appropriate. But Bellinort was not Jules' brother. He was a friend. A handsome friend who was coming to visit which Jules had not thought to mention to Luc.

Perhaps this was how American friendships are? Luc thought, his nostrils flaring. But Bellinort wasn't American. He was French. And Luc knew very well how French men handled friendships with the opposite sex. It was not something a husband would be bound to approve.

He returned the letter and envelope to the book, not caring if it was in the wrong place in the book or that Jules might realize he had read it. He was her husband. They had no secrets.

Or if they did, that stopped now.

He turned and left the bedroom and stepped into the living room where he saw the dirty dishes from last night sitting on the counter. He turned away in disgust and stormed out of the cottage, striding toward the car. He thought about leaving her a note telling her he wouldn't be home for dinner. But as he climbed into his car, still furious, he decided she could probably figure that out for herself.

17

By late afternoon, the sun was hanging lower in the sky, bathing the garden at *La Fleurette* in a soft golden light. A gentle breeze carried the mixed scent of roses and herbs to where I sat in the wicker settee. Justine and Lèa knelt side by side amidst the vegetables, their hands deftly pulling stubborn weeds from the soil. Bees droned lazily from flower to flower. In the distance, I could hear the village church bells signaling the hour.

The day had definitely gotten away from me, and I knew Luc would be home soon. I still didn't have a plan for dinner. I felt a wave of annoyance that collided with guilt at the thought that the meal was my responsibility. Maybe we could go to the village for dinner? I brightened at the thought. It would be a sort of peace offering.

As if she could read my mind, Lèa looked up from her work.

"Why have you not brought Luc over for dinner lately?" she asked.

"He's got a new murder case," I said, evasively.

"Hèlo Montrachet," Justine said, nodding. "We heard."

How in the world they could've heard about his murder when I know for a fact that Luc only found out about it last night was beyond me.

"I don't suppose you heard who killed him?" I asked.

"It could be anyone in the village," Lèa said. "He wasn't a beloved member of the tribe."

"What is that supposed to mean?" I asked. "You went to his shop every week."

"Yes, of course but that is about cheese," Lèa said as if speaking to a dunce.

Naturally. She would've bought cheese from Hitler himself if he was the only nearby source available.

"Okay, so what did he actually do to get the village on his bad side?" I asked.

"He was a braggard for accomplishments he never did," Lèa said.

"He was quite admired, at one point," Justine said.

Lèa gave her a sharp look.

"You exaggerate." She turned back to me. "Let's just say he wasn't always reviled."

"Wow. High praise coming from you, Lèa. Again, what did he do?"

"Nothing. Well, he lost his wife and daughter in a car accident."

I frowned. "And for that the village turned on him?"

"It was how he *reacted* to the tragedy," Lèa said.

"His grief made him bitter," Justine said. "He became harsh and argumentative."

"He was accused of cheating customers," Lèa added.

"Horrors."

"I know you think that is funny," Lèa said severely. "It is your American wit coming to the front again."

"Sorry," I said. "I guess I would've assumed that the

village would've been a little more forgiving. He lost his whole family."

"Not quite. There was a surviving daughter," Justine said.

"Melanie," Lèa said.

"Yes. She left home as soon as she was able," Justine said.

"And since then, Hèlo allowed himself to get swept up in rivalries and feuds with other village families over trivial things. He took sides in disputes," Lèa said.

"Do you know where his daughter is now?"

"I heard she lives in Aix," Justine said.

I knew that by now Luc will have probably gone to Aix to give notice to the daughter of her father's death. Since the EMP we have spent nearly two years with absolutely no technology or communication but in the last year phones were back for the elderly and hospitals. It was possible that Hèlo's daughter might be reachable by phone. But even if she wasn't, a very good friend of mine was reachable and I decided I needed a favor.

Even though he's not elderly or sick, Thibault Theroux was probably the first person in Chabanel to get a phone after the EMP. I called him from the twins' landline to see if he could give me a ride to Aix tomorrow or the day after.

When I hung up, both twins regarded me with excitement at the thought that I might be able to get information about Hèlo's death. It's true what they say about information being the most important commodity there is. And in a world without Netflix or Facebook, that goes double.

18

That night at dinner, it was clear that Luc was still pissed.

He wasn't speaking much and was doing his best not to get eye contact with me. At one point I swear I could hear him grinding his teeth. After my day with the twins, I was in a talky mood, but unfortunately, he wasn't. I'd had hopes that the day apart would have smoothed over the rough edges of our fight the night before. It didn't help that I had no dinner ready for him but only the suggestion that we go out to eat.

"You can't have the Chabanel café as your fallback whenever you don't feel like cooking," he said as he sat at the dining table, his arms crossed. "Or *les soeurs*."

"Speaking of them," I said, determined not to buy into his black mood, "I saw them today and they asked about the cheese seller's death. I guess it's the talk of the town."

He glowered at me.

"Don't pretend you didn't already talk to Matteo about it," he growled. "He told me you followed him into the cheese shop."

Why, that dirty rat.

"I was curious," I said.

"That's no excuse! You could've contaminated the scene. You probably did contaminate the scene!"

I wanted to retort that I'd certainly not contaminated it any more than Matteo had. But I bit my tongue.

"Well, now that you know I was there," I said reasonably, "I need to tell you that I saw a very mysterious man on the street watching the shop."

"Why are you doing this, Jules?" Luc asked in frustration. "Have I not made it clear I don't want you involved in this investigation?"

"Am I supposed to gouge out my eyes if I see something?" I asked tartly. "Am I not supposed to see the things I see? Or just not tell you about them?"

"Why not just add it to the list of other things you do but don't tell me about?" he said, his eyes glittering with anger.

"What are you talking about?"

Now I had my own arms crossed.

"I'm talking about your little friend Davos coming for a visit. When were you going to mention that to me? Or were you?"

I stared at him and then glanced toward the bedroom where Davos' letter was. Unless Luc had spoken to *les soeurs* today—and I was pretty sure he hadn't—he'd read my letter. Immediately I felt heat flushing through my body.

"Just what are you insinuating?" I asked, trying not to overreact.

Who am I kidding? The overreacting part is the best part. It was all I could do not to start screaming. My indignation seemed to take Luc back a bit. I guess he'd wanted to *imply* all manner of evil-doing on my part, but he wasn't ready to come out and accuse me.

"Nothing," he muttered.

"No, out with it!" I shouted. "Did you think I was going to meet Davos on the sly? Maybe sneak off with him while you were at work?"

"I don't know!" he said, raising his voice.

"Seriously?" I shrieked, throwing away all my good intentions to keep my cool.

"Why didn't you tell me he was coming?" he demanded.

"Because I knew you'd act just like this!"

He glared at me and all I could think of was Katrine telling me I should follow my heart and trust that Luc would fall in line.

And then I remembered that Katrine's husband was in jail for trying to murder her and I wondered why in the world I was taking marital advice from her.

19

The next morning, after another quiet night of both of them seething, Luc left again before Jules was awake. Even as upset as he still was, he couldn't resist watching her for a moment while she slept—so beautiful, so peaceful, so non-argumentative. He didn't know why they were so badly out of step these days—although heaven knows it was a characteristic that had virtually defined their relationship as long as they'd known each other.

Now sitting in his office in Chabanel, he was determined to put his marital discord aside for the morning and concentrate on the murder case in front of him. He laid out the six photographs that Matteo had taken of the body in the field and then another twenty Matteo had taken of the cheese shop where it was obvious to anyone with eyes that a struggle had taken place.

I should've been treating this as a crime long before the body was discovered.

Luc felt nausea settle in his stomach. He was screwing up.

The ME's preliminary findings were typed up in a document laying on the desk before him. Luc had skimmed it when he'd first received it and now went back over it more carefully.

Hèlo Montrachet, male, sixty-one years of age.

Luc read the brief description of where the body had been discovered *(lying in a fallow field on the north side of the village along the route d'Eguilles)*. He glanced over at one of the photos of the body. The smiling crescent across Montrachet's throat was clearly visible, lined in crimson from the dried blood. He was struck again by what an odd way that was to kill someone. Matteo had searched the area and had found nothing matching a possible murder weapon.

Luc turned his attention back to the ME's report where the doctor had listed such things as the estimated time of death—based on rigor mortis and core body temperature—as early yesterday evening.

Luc paused in thought. Montrachet had been reported missing two days prior, on a Tuesday. If he died yesterday evening, it meant he'd been kept hostage somewhere before being killed. Luc made a mental note to tell Matteo to start looking for places where the cheese seller could've been held. Possibly one of the many abandoned buildings, which —after the EMP three years ago—had increased in number in the area.

The ME noted zero evidence of a struggle or any defensive wounds on the body. Luc frowned. Had Hèlo been incapacitated in some way? Or was he simply not threatened by his assailant?

Luc stood up and walked to the window. From this vantage point the Café Provencal was in clear view, but he wasn't really seeing anything but the memory of Hèlo Montrachet's body. Montrachet had been found fully clothed with his shoes on and his wallet still in his pocket. The throat wound suggested that he had been attacked from behind. Whether he'd turned his back on his killer, or his assailant had snuck up on him wasn't knowable at this point. Luc sighed and went back to his desk. There had been very little DNA to collect at the scene, but even if there had been, nowadays they had no way of analyzing it.

Then there was the question of the ring. Luc picked up the little baggie from his desk with the ring inside. It looked like a promise ring or perhaps an engagement ring. Luc knew Montrachet had been seeing a woman in Chabanel and he'd sent Matteo to get a statement from her.

Which still didn't answer the question: *why was Hèlo clutching a ring while he was being murdered?*

Luc tossed down the baggie and rubbed a hand over his face. He had put in a request for a toxicology panel to see if Hèlo had been drugged but the results would likely be months away—if ever. Meanwhile, the ME had taken the body to Aix to perform a full autopsy but again, the results of that were not likely to put the period at the end of this sentence until sometime next year.

"Any thoughts?"

Luc jerked his head up to see Matteo standing in his doorway.

"Not really," Luc said. "Not yet," he amended.

"Does it look personal to you?" Matteo asked.

"You mean as opposed to some random killer wandering the countryside?" Luc asked.

Instantly, Luc felt guilty for his snideness. It wasn't professional and he knew Matteo was only trying to be a real detective.

"A random killer doesn't explain why Montrachet was found clutching an engagement ring," Luc said.

"Perhaps he was gay?" Matteo said.

"Is that what you think?" Luc asked, with a sigh.

"Well, I admit it would be a surprise. Hèlo has dated half the women in Chabanel at one time or another."

"It makes more sense that he ripped the ring off his attacker," Luc said.

"Except there's no other sign that he fought back," Matteo said with a frown. "No skin under his nails, no fibers on his clothing, no marks on his knuckles."

"We don't even know if he died in the pasture," Luc said with frustration. "All we know is that he was forcibly taken from his cheese shop."

Matteo nodded solemnly.

"Did you talk to his girlfriend?" Luc asked.

"She wasn't home."

"Keep trying."

After that, Matteo turned and walked away, and Luc was left with a desktop full of photos and absolutely no clue as to how the cheese seller had died. All he really had for sure was a constant buzz in his brain that reminded him that all was not well at home.

20

That morning, as I pedaled down the deserted country lane toward town, a gentle breeze rustled through my hair. A symphony of bird song seemed to fill the air, providing a peaceful soundtrack as I rode along. Everywhere I looked, the vibrant colors of early summer surrounded me, especially the dark red of poppies which blanketed the fields on either side of the road.

As one with nature as I was starting to feel, I still couldn't ignore the unpleasant thrum of discontent in the back of my brain that had Luc's name on it.

He'd sulked the whole evening, after which we'd gone to bed hungry, our backs to each other, angry and stubborn the pair of us. I know he thought I was asleep when he left this morning, but I was really just trying to avoid a morning that began with ugly words. As soon as he left, I got up and got dressed. Since I knew I was going into the village today, I didn't mind that there was nothing to eat for breakfast in the cottage.

Once I crested the final hill, the village came into view, its church spire showing first as it rose above the multicolored terra cotta roofs all aglow in the morning light. I coasted down the last stretch of road to town, already tasting the *café au lait* and fresh-baked croissant I had my heart set on. Once in town, I rode straight for Café Provençal, bypassing the police station without even a head turn in its direction.

I skidded to a stop in front of the café and immediately spotted Katrine on the terrace with her head down and a cup of coffee in front of her on the table. I propped my bike against a nearby post and hurried over toward her.

"Bonjour, Katrine!" I called, startling her.

She looked up at me with the strangest look on her face and I found myself slowing as I approached her table.

"What's the matter?" I asked.

"What?" she said. "Nothing."

"Well, the expression on your face begs to differ."

I dropped my bag on the table and sat down. Immediately Janice, the new café waitress, came over to take my coffee and croissant order. I turned my attention back to Katrine. I could see that she'd been writing in a notebook or journal.

"Seriously," I said. "What's going on?"

Katrine made a face and what could only be called a forced smile.

"It's nothing," she said. "Annabelle had a cough this morning. That's all."

I nodded. I have no children of my own of course, but I know for a parent nothing can ruin a day faster than a sick child.

"I'm sorry to hear that," I said.

"It's nothing. She'll be fine. What about you? How are you and Luc?"

"We're crap, honestly," I said with a sigh as Janice

brought me my coffee and pastry. "We've done nothing but fight since I last saw you."

"Oh, Jules, no."

"So, if he's going to do a major one eighty like you promised me, he's a little behind schedule."

"It'll happen. Hang in there."

"I don't have much choice, do I?"

"How's the property dispute case coming? Do you think you will have a report for me soon?"

"Probably by next week. But on a more interesting subject have you heard anything about the cheese seller?"

Katrine shook her head.

"Only that he'd been killed in a pasture outside of town. It's terrible," she said. "I don't suppose Luc has mentioned anything to you about it?"

"He's silent as a grave on any subject that doesn't include my culinary improvement program," I said, sipping my coffee.

"Oh? How's that going?"

"It's not, Katrine. That was a joke. But listen, I was with Matteo the day after Montrachet went missing and we were looking through his cheese shop—"

"Matteo allowed you to assist him?"

Katrine's mouth fell open in surprise.

"Well, *assist* may not be the right word for it," I said. "But the point is, when I left the shop, I saw this old fellow watching the front of the place. He definitely did not look like he was just walking by."

"What did he look like?"

"Old guy, dressed in clothes that looked too big for him. Long face, shaggy eyebrows."

"That sounds like Monsieur Dubois," Katrine said, nodding. "He's an old friend of Hèlo's."

"That surprises me," I said. "Because he didn't look very concerned. Quite the opposite, in fact. He had a look that was practically evil."

"Well, I heard they had a falling out."

"Really? Do you know why?"

"I do not. But do you know who might?"

"I'm way ahead of you. Madame Gabin."

We both laughed about that and then talked about nothing much until I paid for my coffee and croissant and headed out to the shops to pick up something for dinner tonight. Even though we left on a high note and with a hug, I could tell that there was something about Katrine that was not right. And while it's entirely possible that Annabelle did in fact have a cough, I'm not buying that that's the reason Katrine was acting weird.

Not for a minute.

After I left the café, I went straight to the village market where I wound my way down the bustling alleyway of market stalls. I wandered slowly, basket swinging idly at my side as my thoughts worked overtime. I paused to inspect a bin full of tomatoes, lifting several to sniff. It was the season for good tomatoes, but I knew the twins would be horrified at the thought of my paying good money for them when they were so easy to grow in one's own garden. I put the tomatoes in my basket.

As I continued to walk the outdoor aisles of the market, more discordant ideas and possibilities collided and reformed in my head. And not just about the murder case. I started off wondering what was up with Katrine? And then my thoughts migrated to the murder. I couldn't fathom how the cheese seller went from being dragged out of his cheese shop to ending up in a field nobody ever visited on the northwest side of Chabanel. Was Montrachet's abduction and subsequent murder truly random, or was something else involved? Finally, my thoughts inevitably ended up with my current problems with Luc. I couldn't help but wonder if he had always been so misogynistic, and I'd just not seen it. Or had I seen it and thought it was cute?

I passed by the fishmonger, where strong scents of the sea wafted around me, but I didn't think I was ready to tackle a fish dish yet. By the time my basket was full, I had worked myself into several interlocking mental circles with no apparent solutions. This was the moment I spotted Matteo weaving his way through the market.

I could see he wasn't shopping but heading somewhere. As soon as I saw him, a flood of questions filled my brain and I was bee-lining after him, totally uncaring that the broccoli vendor would be packing up in another thirty minutes.

"Detective Matteo!" I called out. "Matteo!"

I saw him turn, a frown on his face which only deepened when he saw it was me.

"I cannot talk to you," he said, turning around.

"Even if I'm in trouble and need help?" I said as I came even with him.

He gave me an askance look. "Is that true?"

I didn't bother answering.

"What do you know about Monsieur Dubois?" I asked.

"Who?"

"He was a friend of Hèlo Montrachet's," I said. "Only I hear now he's his sworn enemy."

I made up that last part, but it got Matteo to stop moving.

"They are enemies?" he asked.

"That's what I heard," I said. "And I saw him outside the cheese shop when you and I were there yesterday. He was watching the shop."

Matteo looked around as if suddenly worried about the possibility of our being seen together and I reminded myself that he'd already spilled the beans to Luc about my being in the cheese shop—which had probably not gone down well for Matteo.

"Thank you for your information," he said stiffly, and began to turn away.

But I wasn't giving up that easily.

"I also heard Montrachet had a girlfriend," I said. "Did you know that?"

I knew those last four words would be like a red flag to a bull.

"If you are referring to Elise Lefèvre," Matteo said smugly, "I am on my way to take her statement right now."

He looked so proud of himself that I didn't have the heart to tell him that he'd just told me key information that I hadn't known before. I just smiled and nodded as if I'd known the name all along and then turned away to finish my shopping.

As if.

21

An hour later, I was huddled in an empty doorway, across the street from Madame Lefèvre's townhome feeling the morning sun beat down mercilessly on my shoulders. A little gray kitten sat at my feet attacking my shoelaces, and I kept gently nudging it away. The last thing I could do was bring home another cat—either to Luc's place or *La Fleurette*.

While I watched Madame Lefèvre's doorway, I thought I detected the scent of olive trees from the fields on the other side of the tidy row of townhomes. Before the EMP, those fields had sat unharvested for decades. Since then, some enterprising souls were plucking them of their fruit to squeeze and sell at the Sunday markets. And I'd heard doing a decent business.

As I stared at Lefèvre's front door, I had to admit to being mildly surprised that the pudgy sixty-something victim had a girlfriend. I know that's terribly ageist of me, but I've *seen* Hèlo Montrachet in a sleeveless undershirt. Okay, now that's just offensive in a different way.

In any case, I was curious to see what the girlfriend of a dumpy, middle-aged cheese seller looked like. So, sue me.

I'd followed Matteo to Madame Lefèvre's door since that saved me all kinds of time trying to find her address on my own. I didn't love the fact that I'd have to question her after Matteo since I was sure he'd probably offend her in the process thereby making it harder for me to get anything out of her. But I was in luck. She didn't answer the door when he knocked and after a while, Matteo being Matteo, he gave up and walked away.

I stayed in my hiding spot until he was out of sight because I was interested to see if Madame Lefèvre really was out or if she'd give herself away once she thought Matteo was gone. And she did. A curtain in the window on the second floor twitched and a face peered out, looking both ways down the street. I waited a moment longer, so she'd be good and unsuspecting and then made my way across the street.

The front of her townhome was in deep shadow, but I stood close to the door in case she tried looking out the same window when I knocked. To improve my chances of her answering, I sang out: "Free apricot samples!"

Now I can't imagine any fruit vendor in France going door to door handing out free samples, but I guess hope is eternally springing around here because the next thing I heard was the sound of footsteps thundering down the stairs and then the door swung open.

Elise Lefèvre was a thin, angular woman with shoulder-length bleached blonde hair that framed a narrow face marked by deep lines around her mouth and eyes. I'd seen the effects of heavy smoking before; here it had revealed itself in Madame Lefèvre's complexion and left it tinged yellow.

She was dressed casually in loose cotton pants which hung low on her bony hips, topped with an oversized shapeless top. Her overall appearance suggested a woman who prioritized function over form. I tried to imagine her as anyone's mistress—let alone the portly village cheesemaker's—but the image wouldn't gel.

"Bonjour, Madame Lefèvre," I said cheerily, and stretched out my hand with the bunch of micro greens I'd just bought at the market. She frowned at the greens as if registering that they weren't apricots but took them all the same. Before she could close the door, I stepped inside. Instinctively, she moved back to allow me to enter.

"I wanted to tell you how sorry I was for your loss," I said.

She folded her arms across her chest.

"It's about time someone treated me with the respect I deserve," she said bitterly. "I can't believe it's the *American* who has the grace to recognize my position as Hèlo's widow."

I was pretty sure she and Hèlo weren't married so I assume she was conveniently adopting the title in order to fit what she saw as a starring role in the unfolding drama of his murder.

"I know the village will rally around when they've overcome their shock," I said. "I don't suppose you saw Monsieur Montrachet the day he disappeared?"

"No, he was supposed to come by but didn't."

"Did you mention it to anyone when he didn't show?" I asked.

She narrowed her eyes at me.

"How was I to know he was in trouble? And what would I have done if I had known? If the police weren't so useless, they'd know who wanted him dead!"

I felt my heartbeat quicken.

"Yes?" I said. "Who is that?"

"Why, Marie Fournier, of course! She couldn't stand that he chose me over her."

I nodded but I was frowning now. Marie Fournier was gay and the whole village knew it. It wasn't believable that she gave two figs about who Hèlo Montrachet was getting it on with.

"I told him she wasn't right in the head," Elise continued, jabbing an accusatory finger at some unseen target and getting louder and more agitated. "You know her girlfriend left her, right?"

"I didn't know that," I said.

The truth was I hadn't seen Enora in the *boulangerie* or in the village for some time now.

"It's hardly a surprise," Elise said.

"How would Enora Roche leaving Madame Fournier matter to how Hèlo died?"

"Because Madame Fournier killed him, of course," she said loudly, her face reddening. "When her girlfriend left her, Madame Fournier figured it was her chance to get Hèlo."

"But Marie Fournier is gay," I said, wondering if that fact was irrelevant to Madame Lefèvre's conviction that the woman was in love with her boyfriend.

She snorted in disbelief.

"That was all a ruse, of course! But then, there was the matter of the incident."

I was careful to maintain a calm demeanor, but it wasn't easy. This woman was all over the map with her emotions. Mad one minute, affecting grief the next, and downright suspicious of me throughout.

"What was the incident?" I asked.

"Everybody knows about it," she said, waving away my question.

"Great," I said. "Then I'll just ask Madame Fournier or someone who—"

"There's no way *she* will tell you the truth," she said, shaking her head almost violently.

"Okay, well then—"

"Madame Fournier was convinced that Hèlo cheated her out of the shop location where the cheese shop is. She wanted to expand her bakery and put in a bid for the location but Hèlo got it instead."

"How was that cheating her?" I asked.

"Exactly! It was totally above board! But Fournier was convinced that Hèlo had done something underhanded. Trust me, it was Marie Fournier who killed him."

We talked for a few more minutes after that but honestly, the woman soon began to full-on rave only this time accompanied by tears. I wasn't at all sure what part of her tirade I could believe—if any of it. Later, as I was walking back to the center of town, I tried to sort what I'd learned and decided it was very little. While on the face of it, Madame Lefèvre *had* suggested a possible suspect, first, it was a suspect with two totally opposing motives, and second, it was someone who was confined to a wheelchair. I walked down the front walk to find my way back to the center of the village.

22

After my visit with Elise Lefèvre, I made my way to the *boulangerie* to pick up bread for tonight as well as for the twins and of course to see if I couldn't talk to Marie Fournier to get any information that might explain in greater detail what Madame Lefèvre had just told me.

As I pushed open the door to the *boulangerie*, the little bell over the door heralded my presence. I was surprised to see that there were no customers in the bakery—nothing but a vacant interior filled with shelves lined with fresh loaves of wonderful smelling bread. In the back, I could see Marie Fournier energetically wheeling around where I imagined all the mixing bowls and pan and ovens were. When I stepped up to the counter, I could almost feel the heat radiating from the ovens.

"Bonjour!" I called out.

The beaded curtains behind the counter rippled open and Marie Fournier appeared, propelling her wheelchair forward with practiced efficiency. She had flour dusting the deep blue apron that covered her ample figure. I always say don't trust a skinny baker. Marie Fournier might be a Class-A grump, but she definitely tasted her own wares. That's an endorsement I can get behind.

When she came forward, I couldn't help but notice that her arms were strong and muscled from wheeling herself about and kneading the heavy bread dough. She steered herself up to the counter, wiping her hands on a cloth on her lap.

"Bonjour, Madame DeBray," she said with a frown. "What can I do for you?"

Her face was pinched as if it physically pained her to have to inquire what I wanted.

"I just need a few things for dinner tonight," I said. "Two *baguettes* and maybe some chocolate croissants for tomorrow's breakfast."

She swiveled around to pull the *baguettes* out of a tall wicker basket on the counter.

"You should buy the pastries the day you will eat them," she said. "They will be stale otherwise."

"Yeah, in a perfect world," I said, smiling as she wrapped the *baguettes*.

"Will that be all?" she asked.

I guess she really wasn't going to let me have any pastries unless I promised to eat them today.

"Sure," I said as she pushed the *baguettes* across the counter to me. "I wanted to say that I'm sorry about your accident. I only recently heard what happened."

I stopped talking so that she could fill in the details of what had happened, but Marie Fournier was an odd duck and she clamped her mouth shut stubbornly and crossed her arms.

"You must be very upset about what happened to Hèlo Montrachet," I said, trying again.

"Why must I?" she asked.

"Well, because you share a street with him. You're both shop owners. I imagine you must have known each other for years."

"I know that Hèlo Montrachet was a cheat and a liar," she said. "And that the world is better off without him. Will that be all? I have a tray of *fougasse* rising in the back."

And with that, she swiveled her chair around, her strong arms pushing her back through the beaded curtain and disappeared into the back room.

23

My bike ride home that afternoon was a miserable one since the rain that had held off all day decided to unload at the very moment I was surrounded by highway with no trees or sheltering overhangs anywhere in sight. I'd originally intended to drop the bread off at *les soeurs* but since they were a good two miles further on from Luc's place, I chose to believe that they'd probably baked bread today and I drove straight to Luc's cottage, arriving soaked and out of sorts.

I'd had the full unpleasant bike ride to think about what I'd learned from both Madame Lefèvre and Marie Fournier. If you eliminate the content of what the two women said and just focused on their manner, I must say you get a pretty interesting picture. I'm not sure there's an investigative school in the world that would ever suggest doing this, but I have had great luck with it.

Take Elise Lefèvre. If I only paid attention to what she'd *said*, I'd have missed that the *way* she said it was equally as telling if not more so. She accused Marie Fournier of killing Hèlo but her affect appeared to be about making sure I knew that she was grieving. What does that reveal to me? When a significant other isn't really sorry that her beloved is dead? That she was trying to point the finger at other people? Yeah, that looks like guilt to me. Of course, the problem with that theory is the fact that we know Hèlo was assaulted in his cheese shop and dragged out, killed somewhere else and then taken to the abandoned field and dumped. There was no way Madame Lefèvre—not even a hundred pounds soaking wet—could have done any part of that three-step process.

And Marie Fournier? Well, she seemed pretty unbalanced to me overall. Again, if you take away the specifics of the content of what she said—that Hèlo cheated her and she hated him—and instead pay attention to *how* she said it...well, no, it still comes out as her looking nuts. But much like Madame Lefèvre—only more so—I can't see Marie Fournier assaulting, dragging and dumping Hèlo from a wheelchair. How would she have gotten to the pasture? With a body? No, the idea of the baker getting the body out to the countryside was unimaginable. But as I have the experience to say—that doesn't mean it didn't happen.

Once home, I stripped off my outerwear of sopping clothing and hung them on chair backs to dry while I put away the bits of meat and produce that I'd brought home for dinner. In the end, I'd ended up buying a rotisserie chicken with a few salad items that didn't require cooking. I knew Luc had his heart set on me cooking and not just compiling dinner, but I do think that's a slippery slope. What next? Grow the asparagus from a seed before steaming it and drenching it in butter I churned from cream? I'm just saying that getting his hopes up might not be the best way forward.

After toweling off my hair, I set about cleaning the rocket lettuce and what microgreens I hadn't given to Elise

Lefèvre. By the time I heard Luc's car pull into the gravel drive, I had the table set, the candles lit, and the food on the table. Even I had to admit that the dinner looked pretty good.

∼

That night, Luc and I were both trying really hard to make up for last night. I'd bent over backwards—once more—to present a nice meal. I even put a small vase of poppies on the table. Luc seemed genuinely delighted about the effort I'd gone to and by the time we sat down to it, there was a real lack of tension between us for the first time in days. After my afternoon spent interviewing Marie Fournier and Elise Lefèvre, I was dying to talk to him about the Montrachet case. But when I hinted at it, I could feel him tense up, so I dropped it.

I have to say I blamed myself for that. After all, if the only thing we have in common is talking about murder investigations, then that's on me. Luc is doing everything he can to make our relationship about more than work. And I appreciate that. In fact, as I sat there smiling at him from across the table and recognizing how hard he was trying to be talkative and engaging about virtually *nothing*, I found myself seeing all those things in him that I loved: his loyalty, his convictions, his warmth. I felt my heart open up to him.

"You'll never believe what happened at the market today when I was buying the chicken," I said with a laugh. "Madame Lavoie was there as usual with her gang of chickens clucking around her feet. When I asked which bird she recommended, they all started squawking super loud, as if trying to campaign for the job, you know?"

Luc grinned.

"But then two of the chickens got in a fight over it! I mean, they were both flapping their wings and pecking at each other while Madame Lavoie was trying to break it up. There were feathers flying everywhere. So naturally, a crowd gathered to watch the spectacle."

Luc laughed, his eyes crinkling with merriment.

"Well, I only hope they were fighting over who got to be delicious and not who had to be eaten," he said. "But whoever won, this is delicious and, may I say, cooked to perfection."

The smile began to slip from my face.

"Well, that's just it," I said. "I decided I didn't have the heart to disappoint either of the chickens."

He was still grinning at my words but now a look of confusion had begun in his eyes.

"So, I went next door to the *charcuterie*," I said. "And *voila*."

He looked at his plate, fork and knife still in his hands.

"This is an already cooked chicken?" he asked.

It was the way he said it. He wasn't marveling that something from the store could taste so much like home-made since, let's face it, this is France. Store-bought tastes as good as homemade. No, that's not what he was asking at all.

"It's a rotisserie chicken from the *charcuterie*," I said, my voice icy even though I was still sort of smiling. "If that's what you're asking."

"I see," he said and then put down his fork. "Well, baby steps, I guess."

I literally felt a pounding in my ears. I paused only a moment before standing up from the table and walking to the bedroom where I quietly packed a small suitcase. As I put underthings, jeans and blouses into the bag, my throat felt dry from my attempts to control my breathing and stay calm. I wasn't surprised that Luc didn't come looking for me. I'm not sure what he thought I was doing in the bedroom. Maybe he wasn't even curious. Maybe he thought I was so ashamed of presenting him with a pre-cooked chicken that I couldn't face him and I was in here sobbing my heart out. By the time I walked back out to the dining room, the dishes were still on the table, and he was in the living room reading the paper. I stood for a moment until he looked up and saw me.

"What's happening?" he asked, slowly getting to his feet, his eyes on the suitcase in my hand.

"This is me taking baby steps," I said.

And that's exactly what I took, right out the door.

24

The next morning, I was up early bouncing along in the passenger seat of Thibault's old 2CV, my stomach soured from too much coffee and not enough breakfast. It had rained in the night and the road in front of us seemed to be actually steaming. Thibault was in a good mood—so much so that he didn't seem to notice that I wasn't talking much.

My thoughts were swirling around my brain in overdrive. A part of me felt like I'd massively overreacted to Luc's comment about the rotisserie chicken last night. The more I thought about it, the more it sounded like the kind of stupid fights newlyweds get into. But on the other hand, from the minute I walked out of his cottage until I arrived at *La Fleurette* I didn't hesitate, I didn't have second thoughts, I didn't consider turning around. In fact, when I got to *La Fleurette*—in spite of the supremely disappointed looks on both sisters' faces—I was never so relieved to be anywhere. I knew the twins wanted details about what had happened, but I was weary and heartsick and so went straight upstairs to my old bedroom, Cocoa at my heels, and slept until I heard Thibault honking his horn outside my window this morning.

"I didn't expect you to be at *La Fleurette* now that you are married," he said. "*Les soeurs* called me this morning to tell me to pick you up there."

I was grateful they had thought to call him since I hadn't.

"Well, it's a modern marriage," I said. "Luc and I do all kinds of things differently."

"Well, living apart would definitely be different," he said.

I turned to look at Thibault who had something unidentifiable trapped in his beard that waggled as he talked and which I found moderately distracting. I've known Thibault for the entire time I've lived in Provence. He's always been unfailingly helpful to both me and the twins—and honestly, anyone else who needs his help—and yet I still flinch when I first see him. Unctuous, gangly, unkempt, and yes, with food usually parked in some part of his straggling beard, Thibault is a big lug of a guy with beady eyes and hair that never looks washed. But he's a dear man with a big heart and one of my closest friends in Chabanel.

"I found out that the woman I need to talk to lives at Les Jardins de Provence apartments," I said, deciding to change the subject. "She's a teacher so she should be home."

"She is not expecting you?"

"I'm pretty sure she doesn't have a phone," I said defensively.

"So this is an ambush," he said cheerfully.

I suppose it was my angry exodus from Luc's place last night that had me in a sour mood, but I didn't appreciate Thibault's sardonic spin on my errand today. It's true Melanie Montrachet wasn't expecting me, but since she was newly grieving the loss of her father, I was hoping she might be open to talking to someone. Honestly, I wasn't sure I was going to find out anything important but if this had been *my* murder case, she would definitely be one of the boxes I'd be ticking.

A few minutes later we were driving down Cours Mirabeau, the main street in Aix. Everywhere I looked I saw people strolling with their dogs, walking solo or hand in hand. The outdoor cafés were crammed full of people drinking coffee. Aix's trademark golden yellow buildings with their blue shutters and black wrought-iron Juliette balconies lined up on both sides of the Cours. As in Chabanel, the buildings were made mostly of limestone in hues that ranged from lemon yellow to golden ochre. When the Provençal sunlight hit them from any angle, they looked like they were glowing.

Although many of the shops in town were closed with boards nailed across their windows, a surprising number were still open, including every single bakery and *pâtisserie* we passed. Once we reached Place Richelme, I saw the food market was being dismantled in order to set out café tables for the afternoon. The cobblestones underneath the tables were wet where merchants had hosed down the street in front of their booths.

"Let me out," I said to Thibault. "Her apartment is right there."

Thibault pulled his car over. Unlike the old pre-EMP days, available parking spots were no longer an issue in Aix. I hopped out of the car as soon as he stopped.

"Where will you be?" I asked.

He nodded at where the café tables were being set up.

"Great," I said before turning and heading for the apartment building across the street.

25

I'd easily found Melanie Montrachet's address yesterday during a very quick stop in the midst of my village grocery shopping at the Chabanel City Hall—a little chore that used to be handled on the Internet but now needed to be done with shoe leather. I knew from experience that the mayor's office would have a list of all government workers in the area—especially schoolteachers, which the twins told me they believed Melanie was. Even if she was no longer teaching, there was a good chance she still lived at the address where she'd registered when she was teaching.

The aging apartment building I had Thibault drop me in front of was set awkwardly on a narrow side street in the old quarter of Aix off Place Richelme. Its faded stone facade was covered in patches of crumbling plaster, and it was stained from years of exposure to the elements. Like the nicer buildings on Cours Mirabeau though, it had wrought-iron balconies. But unlike on the Cours, these balconies jutted out irregularly from the upper floors, and were overflowing with hanging laundry and potted plants, or just rusted and empty.

I pushed open the heavy entrance door to reveal a dark entryway with flickering overhead lights. At least there was electricity, I thought. These days that wasn't always a given. The floor tiles were worn and cracked, and the stairwell smelled musty. As I headed toward the stairs, I heard voices filtering through the thin walls. Aix is a medieval city with cobblestone streets that hark back to the fourteen hundreds when Aix was the capital of Provence. Except for the Apple Store and a couple shops in the underground mall, everything here is extremely old. But this building brought the term *antiquity* to new meaning. I was literally unsure if my foot would go through the treads as I climbed the stairs.

Once I reached the top floor, I walked down a narrow hall under a precarious, sagging water-stained ceiling until I came to the number on the address I had. I knocked on the door and immediately heard the rabid yapping of a small dog inside. Within moments, the door opened.

I'm not sure what I was expecting but this wasn't it. Hèlo Montrachet was short and pudgy, but his daughter was tall —very tall—and trim, almost gaunt. Her hair was pulled back into a tight bun, and she was wearing leggings with athletic shoes and a form-fitting tunic top. Clearly exercise was important to her.

"Madame Montrachet?" I asked.

She was holding a small scruffy dog in her arms and looking at me suspiciously—well, both of them were actually. But a cold welcome is not unusual in France. Not even pre-EMP days to be fair. It didn't mean she wouldn't thaw. But especially without phones to give a person a heads-up, a surprise visit from a stranger was always reason for wariness if not downright suspicion.

"I am Jules DeBray," I said. "I live in Chabanel."

As soon as I mentioned the village where her father had his cheese shop, Melanie's face darkened.

"I wanted to extend my condolences," I said quickly. "For your loss."

"That is not necessary," she said in a low, gruff voice. "My father and I weren't close."

"I'm sorry to hear that. I was wondering if the police gave you any information on how your father passed?"

"They said someone killed him," she said with a snort. "Big surprise."

"Had you not seen him in a while?"

"I saw him at my mother's funeral although I can't believe he had the nerve to show up. In case you can't tell, I'm glad he's dead."

"I'm sorry. It sounds like it was a difficult relationship."

"Not as difficult as living with him. Do you know when the will is going to be read?"

"Your father's lawyer should call you about that," I said.

"Do you have his name?"

"Me? No, sorry."

"Who are you again?"

"My name is Jules DeBray. I'm the Chabanel police chief's wife. Coming around to talk in person with the bereaved is one of the...one of my duties as his wife."

She snorted loudly again. "And you're English?"

"American."

"Even worse."

Obviously, she wasn't interested in being friends so I figured I might as well go straight for what I'd come for.

"Can you tell me where you were two nights ago around sixteen hundred hours?" I asked.

She made an even uglier face than she'd been wearing

before, and I swear her little dog lifted his lip at me as if he could feel his mistress's animosity through her arms.

"Are you asking me if I have an alibi?" she asked blinking rapidly as if incredulous.

"I'm pretty sure my husband the police chief will get around to asking the same question as soon as he thinks you're no longer in mourning," I said, pleasantly, "which let's face it, you're not."

That's when she slammed the door in my face. Sighing, I turned to make my way back down the smelly hallway. By the time I reached the ground floor, I wasn't at all sure what I'd learned. The fact that she hated her father didn't mean she killed him. The fact that she lived in near poverty did give her motive for wanting whatever he was going to leave her when he died. In France there's never a question about who gets left what when a person dies. The State makes sure that the children get it all, even over the spouse. And Melanie *had* asked about the will.

I found Thibault sipping a *noisette* at one of the cafés that bordered Place Richelme. I signaled to a waiter to bring me one too and sat down at his table.

"That was fast," he said.

"She didn't invite me in."

"*Quelle surprise.*"

"It was probably a waste of time. I thought it was interesting, though, that she was so tall. I guess the mother must have been tall because I don't think Hèlo was even five foot five inches."

"Your point?"

"I'm pretty sure Mademoiselle Montrachet could have manhandled her father out of his store and into the back of a donkey cart."

Thibault looked at me askance.

"Is that how the police think Monsieur Montrachet was taken from the shop? In a donkey cart?"

The waiter came and set down my espresso.

"They are not sharing their theories with me," I said.

"Oh, so this is just *your* theory?"

"Well, there was a struggle in his shop and his body ended up in a pasture a half mile away, so you connect the dots. Either he was dragged there, or he went willingly—except nothing about how his shop looked said he went willingly—or he was somehow conveyed there."

"I don't even know of any donkeys around Chabanel."

"Okay, Thibault," I said testily. "It was just an offhand comment. No real research went into it."

"Clearly. So, you think the daughter killed her own father?"

"You should have heard her, Thibault. All she cared about was the money. Do you know if Hèlo had much to leave?"

Thibault shrugged and signaled to the waiter for our bill.

"He must have," he said. "He only sold cheese, and he never went anywhere. You are aware of the love affair between the French and cheese?"

I smiled in spite of myself.

"Yes, Luc is pretty infatuated with a very flirty little Stilton at the moment."

"You and Luc are quarreling?"

"We're fine. We're just working some kinks out."

"Kinks are often good in a marriage."

"Says the confirmed bachelor."

After that we got back in his car and drove back to Chabanel. I wanted to stop by the *boulangerie* to pick up bread for dinner tonight at *La Fleurette*. We listened to music on Thibault's radio while we drove which I was glad for. I'd started to feel a little embarrassed again about leaving Luc's place last night. I was definitely feeling second thoughts and most of those second thoughts had me massively overreacting to Luc's criticism.

How were we going to solve anything as a couple if we didn't communicate about the things that bothered us? I shouldn't have stormed off—as satisfying as that felt. Instead, I should have told Luc how I felt. I should have told him that I didn't consider myself the dedicated cook within the marriage. I needed to ask him if he was going to be able to accept that.

Luc and I had skirted this issue a few times and what I'd gotten back from him was something along the lines of *if you really loved me, you'd learn to cook*. I think because I didn't want to honestly respond to that request, I'd basically just ignored it. Now I needed for him to see that that the desire to please went two ways. I didn't mind trying to cook if that really did light his jets to have me do it, but I was afraid that his wanting me to was a manifestation of a deeper issue between us. If he was content for me to cook now and then, that was fine. But if he truly thought it was my role in the marriage, then we had a problem. I guess it was better to know now rather than five years from now after I'd run home to mother—i.e. *les soeurs*—a few hundred times.

As we pulled into the village, I saw Luc and Matteo standing outside the police station.

"I wonder what's going on?" Thibault said.

Luc stepped into the street and raised his hands to stop our car. For one mad moment, my heart fluttered in my chest as I thought that he was about to make a grand romantic gesture. Something along the lines of: *Stop, my love. I cannot live without you, and I don't care if the whole village knows it or if you never cook.*

Thibault stopped the car and Luc came to the driver's side window. I wet my lips and prepared to look surprised when he leaned into the window to make his ardent declaration—although even then I did think it would've made more sense for him to come around to my side of the car.

"Thibault Theroux," Luc intoned as he held up a pair of handcuffs. "I'm going to need you to get out of the car."

Even *then* I didn't truly get what was happening. I still thought Luc was in the process of doing some big dramatic expression of apology to me. But it was confusing. Why was he involving Thibault?

"What's going on, DeBray?" Thibault asked, not turning the car off.

Just then, my car door opened, and I felt Matteo put a hand on my arm as if to hold me in place or to pull me out. I wasn't sure which.

"What's going on," Luc said as he reached in, turned off the ignition and jerked open Thibault's car door, "is that I'm arresting you for the murder of Hèlo Montrachet."

26

I stared in stupefaction at the scene unfolding before me.

With a strength I had no idea he had, Luc yanked Thibault out of the car, causing the big man to stumble as Luc swiftly clicked the handcuffs onto his hands.

Then Luc quickly began to inform Thibault of his rights as he hauled Thibault away from the car, past the growing crowd of curious village onlookers. Thibault looked as astonished as I felt—which has to be the only explanation for how Luc was able to manhandle him out of the car since Thibault outweighed him by fifty pounds.

I pushed past Matteo and barreled around the front of the vehicle toward Luc and Thibault.

"What are you doing?" I screeched as I grabbed Luc's arm. "Have you gone mad?"

I realize in hindsight that that probably wasn't the best opening I could've had if I had any hope of cooler heads prevailing—or of Luc not digging in his heels, which he promptly did.

"Stand back, Jules," he ordered. "I'm not explaining this to you in the street."

"It's all right, Jules," Thibault said—amazingly the only one of the three of us who was keeping calm. "I'm sure it is a misunderstanding."

"Misunderstanding?" I said loudly, my nails biting into the palms of my hands to keep from hitting something. "More like jealousy on the part of our police chief!"

Again, you'd think I'd realize how much worse I was making things and how Luc's pride might not be able to withstand too much more battering. But again, no.

"You're doing this just to get back at me," I said loudly, running now to keep up with them as I followed them into the station. "It's petty and mean-spirited!"

"Be quiet, Jules," Luc said over his shoulder.

I could see by how red the back of his neck was, that Luc was now nearly as furious as I was. He stopped at Madame Gabin's desk and waited for Matteo to join him.

"Book him," Luc muttered to Matteo as I came to stand between him and Thibault.

"I am this man's acting counsel," I said, trying to keep my voice calm when what I wanted to do was slap Luc across the face.

"You're not legally qualified to do so," Luc said, not looking at me, as Matteo marched Thibault away to the cells at the back of the station.

He was right about that. I wasn't qualified. But I knew that if I wanted to free Thibault—assuming Luc couldn't be talked out of this arrest—I would need all the information and facts that a lawyer of his would legally be entitled to.

"What evidence do you have against my client?" I asked Luc.

"You need to stay out of this, Jules," Luc growled. "You're making it worse."

"Funny, that's exactly what I was going to say to you," I said. "On two different fronts. So I repeat, what evidence do you have?"

I was keenly aware that Madame Gabin was listening to every juicy word between us and that soon the entire village would get a significantly expanded rendition of this drama. Knowing that made me even angrier—if that was possible.

"Thibault Theroux is the only person within a ten-mile radius who owns a car," Luc said. "He is the only one who knew the victim and who could have moved the body from the cheese shop to the field."

"That's your evidence?" I asked, shaking my head in disbelief "By that token, *you* are a suspect too since you also have a car."

"You are making things worse, Jules," Luc repeated under his breath, almost like a mantra.

"Worse for who?" I asked, glancing at Madame Gabin.

I was surprised she wasn't taking notes. But then again, she wasn't known for the accuracy of her gossip.

"Is that all you have?" I asked him testily.

Luc turned to me, and I could see the full brunt of his humiliation and building fury in his eyes. For me to embarrass him like this in front of Madame Gabin was the height of betrayal. I knew that. I could see that. I still couldn't stop.

"Fine," he said steely. "You want more? Thibault's prints were found on a ring the victim was found clutching."

And on that ominous note, he turned on his heel and walked away.

27

I remained standing in the waiting room between Madame Gabin's desk and the hall where Luc had disappeared. I felt as stunned as if Luc had hit me with a two by four.

Thibault's fingerprints were on something the dead man was clutching?

How was that possible?

I turned slowly toward the door. Luc had closed himself up in his office and Matteo was guarding the hallway to the cells. It was just as well. I needed to think. I went outside and stood on the front steps of the station for a moment. I knew I had to find answers to counter the evidence that Luc thought he had against Thibault, but first I needed to clear my head which at the moment was pounding with confusion and fury.

Luc had left the keys in Thibault's car, so I climbed in and drove slowly out of the village. I say *slowly* since Thibault's car was a stick shift and I hadn't driven one since my driver's ed days in high school. Thankfully, since I was the only car on the road for about a hundred miles, there was no chance of a traffic incident as I made my way home to *La Fleurette*.

As soon as I pulled into the driveway, Cocoa bounded out from the bushes to greet me. But even after a big furry hug and a few well-placed licks, I felt defeated when I walked through the front door. Immediately Justine met me with a questioning look in her eyes.

"What has happened?" she asked.

"Luc arrested Thibault for the murder of Hèlo Montrachet," I said dispiritedly.

Lèa entered the room with a basket of wet laundry in her hands.

"That is ridiculous," she said. "Luc must be suffering under a serious hardship to have done such a mad thing."

Really? I wanted to say. *You're blaming me for this?*

"Make up with him, *chérie*," Justine said as she led me into the kitchen. "And I am sure he will release Thibault immediately."

"I don't know," I said. "I said a few things when he arrested Thibault that might make it hard for him to back down."

Lèa snorted loudly.

"Always you are making things worse," she said. "He is a man, no? He has pride?"

"Why are you always cutting him slack?" I asked crossly as Justine poured me a mug of coffee. "Why don't I ever get the benefit of the doubt?"

"Do you really want me to answer that?" Lèa asked. "Or would you rather just whine and feel sorry for yourself?"

"Enough," Justine said as she saw me getting ready to rip into Lèa. "Tell us what evidence has made him arrest Thibaut."

I sipped the hot coffee and took a moment to calm myself.

"He says only Thibault had the means to get Montrachet from the cheese shop to the field."

"He has a point," Lèa said.

"And he says Thibault's fingerprints were on a ring that was found in Montrachet's hand at the murder site."

"*Vraiment?*" Justine asked with surprise and then clucked her tongue in distress.

"There has to be an explanation for that," I said. "You know Thibault didn't kill Montrachet."

Lèa shrugged.

"We like Thibault," she said. "He has been immensely helpful to us. But of course, we do not know that he didn't kill him."

I literally felt a tic forming in my cheek at her words. In an effort to distract me from throttling Lèa, Justine leaned forward and tapped my hand.

"Who else do you think could have killed Hèlo?"

"Well," I said, "there's Hèlo's best friend Dagnier Dubois who acted shifty when Matteo and I were searching the cheese shop."

"That is all?" Justine said with a frown. "No evidence?"

"*Acting shifty* could be laid at the feet of half the people in Chabanel," Lèa added pointedly.

"Okay, well, then there's Marie Fournier. I'm told she hated Montrachet."

"The crippled baker?" Lèa said, making a face to indicate what she thought of that suggestion.

"Okay, I know it sounds mad," I said. "But how is it that last year she was walking around her bakery making sourdough *batons*, and now she's in a wheelchair but nobody seems to know why or how?"

"I heard it was a horseback riding accident," Justine said.

I frowned.

"I don't believe it," I said. "What was she doing riding a horse? And whose horse?"

As far as I knew Monsieur Dellaux had the only horse in the area, and I think he would've mentioned it if he'd let Marie Fournier get on its back.

"And if it *was* a horseback riding accident," I said, "how come she wasn't in the hospital?"

"She was, *chérie*," Justine said. "It happened when you and Luc were in Paris for your honeymoon."

"What was her injury?"

"I heard it was something about her spine," Lèa said.

"Yes, that's right," Justine said to her sister. "That's what I heard too."

I didn't know why they were being so deliberately ambiguous, but it was clear to me that there was more to the story.

"What difference does it make how she ended up in the wheelchair?" Lèa said, compressing her lips together in a show of barely controlled impatience. "You can't think *she* was physically able to commit the murder."

"Anyone else, *chérie*?" Justine asked.

"Well, I talked to his daughter in Aix today," I said. "Melanie Montrachet. She hated her father, and she looks plenty capable of killing him."

"A daughter to kill her father?" Lèa said with a frown. "Not believable. Who else?"

I threw my hands up in frustration.

"Matteo told me Hèlo had a girlfriend," I said. "Her name is Elise Lefèvre. I met her yesterday and she was super upset about Montrachet's death. Maybe not grief-stricken, but still upset. She seemed to think Marie Fournier could've done it."

"But again, *chérie*," Justine said, "Madame Fournier is crippled."

"You found nothing suspicious about Madame Lefèvre?" Lèa asked.

I looked at her in surprise.

"Are you serious? I'd have to say she's the only one I talked to who *isn't* suspicious," I said. "She wasn't married to him. She couldn't inherit. What was her motive?"

The twins exchanged a cryptic look.

"Okay, what's the look for?" I said. "What do you guys know?"

"Nothing, *chérie*," Justine said. "And it is important not to judge someone based on gossip alone."

"What kind of gossip?" I asked.

"It is not gossip, Justine," Lèa pointed out. "Not if it is true."

"What?" I pressed. "If what's true?"

"Elise Lefèvre has been married twice before," Justine said.

"That's not really a crime," I said.

"Of course not," Justine said. "Except that both her husbands died under mysterious circumstances."

28

Luc sat at his kitchen table, a bottle of wine before him. It was long past eight o'clock, but the air still felt thick and oppressive, as if it were holding the day's heat in a suffocating embrace that not even the open windows could alleviate. A fly droned somewhere in the room.

He stared at the plate in front of him. Whatever had compelled him to stop and pick up a rotisserie chicken for dinner? Especially after it had served as the catalyst for the fight last night! He pushed the plate away, his appetite stolen by the memory of the argument with Jules. He poured himself another glass of wine. He might never eat rotisserie chicken again.

He reran the morning in his mind, remembering how he'd felt as he stood in the street waiting for Thibault and Jules to arrive. An earlier phone call to the twins had confirmed that the two were together after a day of shopping in Aix. He knew of course that Jules was good friends with Thibault but surely, she could see that Luc was only doing his job?

He re-played Jules' words in his head.

"You're doing this just to get back at me. It's petty and mean-spirited!"

They were words spoken in anger and frustration, each syllable a stinging assault. He was working a murder case! Jules of all people should understand! Arresting Thibault wasn't personal. He got up and walked across the room, momentarily too restless and discomfited by the memory of her words. The hard fact was that he was committed to finding the truth about what happened to the cheese seller. It was his job!

He dragged a hand through his hair and felt his shoulders slump. The only problem with that was that he was beginning to seriously doubt that arresting Thibault was truly the best way to that end.

On impulse, he turned and picked up the mobile phone that he'd brought in from the car and dialed the landline number at *La Fleurette*.

"*Allo?*" Justine said when she answered the phone.

"*Allo*, Justine," Luc said. "Is she there?"

"She has had a tiring day," Justine said in as cold a voice as Luc had ever remembered hearing from the usually warm and welcoming woman.

"Has she gone to bed already?" he asked.

"No, Luc," Justine said. "But she has nothing to say to you at the moment."

He rubbed an agitated hand across his face but before he could say any more, Lèa came on the line.

"Do you know her at all?" she asked him angrily.

"I know, I know," he said, although he really didn't. "Can you just have her call me when she calms down?"

"We will relay the message," Lèa said. "But don't even think of showing up here until she is ready to see you."

She hung up then. Luc sighed heavily. The twins were always on his side. Or at least they always had been. He knew from recent conversations with them that they agreed with him that Jules needed to make more of an effort to learn to cook and take care of him. They were on his side!

Right up to the moment when they weren't.

He imagined that arresting Thibault had been a red flag for the twins, who loved the strange man fiercely and unconditionally. If Luc had wanted to keep the twins in his court, he probably shouldn't have accused Thibault of murder.

Even if he's guilty?

He rubbed on his face harder as if to erase the thought that he might have arrested Thibault out of spite just as Jules had accused him. The twins were usually a pretty fair barometer of proper behavior in any given situation. If they thought he'd taken a misstep, there was a good chance he had. On the other hand, Jules was emotional and passionate and often wrong. She spoke before she engaged her brain so many times.

But maybe not this time.

If I want to keep her in my life, I need to stop competing with her or arguing every point with her.

It occurred to him that letting Thibault go was probably the first step to showing Jules that he was willing to compromise. In fact, what a clear cut demonstration of his willingness to bend! As that thought formed and began to develop, he felt a jolt of clarity pierce his brooding gloom. He picked up his wine glass and drank from it, setting the glass down firmly, the clink against the wooden table sounding definitive, like a punctuation to his decision. A weight seemed to lift from his shoulders. He'd been premature in arresting Thibault. Jules was right. He'd allowed his resentment to build an unnecessary barrier between them and now he was going to do the right thing and back down. She'd respect him for that.

He glanced at the chicken on his plate where the remnants of his solitary dinner still lay, and felt the first genuine stirrings of peace.

Maybe we will laugh about this on our ten-year wedding anniversary. Maybe we will always pick up rotisserie chicken as our inside joke and our commitment not to let the little things derail us and our marriage.

A small, tentative smile began to curve the corners of his mouth as he imagined all the possibilities that this first step would bring—including children. The bitterness that had soured the taste of the chicken began to dissipate.

Just then his phone rang, and he felt his pulse quicken thinking it must be Jules calling back. He answered quickly.

"This is Luc," he said breathlessly, eager to share with her his contrition and newfound hope for their future.

"Matteo here, Chief. I went through Thibault's apartment and found something."

Luc felt his stomach begin to roil. He dragged a hand through his hair.

"It's a wire that matches what the ME drew as the possible murder weapon," Matteo said.

"That's all?" Luc said, feeling the tension relax in his shoulders. "Everyone knows Thibault is a hoarder. A wire found in his apartment—"

"There were no prints on it, Chief. It had been wiped clean."

Luc sat down heavily, still holding the phone to his ear.

Why would it have been wiped clean?

Unless it had been used in a murder.

"Chief?"

"Did you bag it?" Luc asked, his voice hoarse.

But he didn't hear Matteo's response. All he heard ringing in his brain was the very real possibility that Thibault had in fact killed Montrachet. Whatever the reasons for that would come out eventually. They always did. But it didn't matter. He knew that even if he had the best evidence in the world—even if Thibault *confessed*—the fact was, Jules would never forgive him for this.

29

The next morning, I was on the road early heading back to Chabanel. I have to say that the sheer ease of just hopping in a car for the two-mile trip to town was going to make giving up that car a major life crisis for me. In any event, after hearing what the twins had to say last night about Madame Lefèvre, I felt as if I had a little better case to lay before Luc and I was excited to do that.

It occurred to me that Luc might be aware that Elise Lefèvre could possibly have killed off two husbands—I needed to make sure I didn't phrase it like that—but he needed to know that I knew it too. I've learned from experience that presenting facts and letting the other person make the obvious deduction is always more convincing than any argument I could make with the same set of facts.

Once I got to Chabanel, I parked out front of the police station next to Luc's Citroen. The second I stepped through the front door I was hit with the luscious scent of fresh-brewed coffee. I really hoped that Thibault was getting some of that. I walked up to Madame Gabin's desk.

"I'm here to see the chief," I said.

"I'm not sure he's in," she said.

"I saw his car outside," I said, trying to keep my voice civil, "so I'm pretty sure he is."

She walked to the edge of the waiting room and stuck her head around the corner.

"Chief! Your wife is here to see you."

I took a measure of comfort in the fact that she was still referring to me as his wife.

"Go on in," she said as she came back to her desk.

I walked down the hall to Luc's office where he sat drinking coffee. I have to say he looked terrible. Stubble darkened his jawline and dark circles were visible under both eyes which were bloodshot from lack of sleep. His hair stuck up at odd angles, probably from repeatedly running his hands through it in frustration and he was wearing the same clothes he had on the day before. A pang of sadness shot through me at his appearance. In fact, all the annoyance and anger I'd felt up to now seemed to melt away seeing the man I loved so clearly unhappy.

"Good morning," he said formally.

"I have new evidence," I said, which wasn't precisely true, but it was new to me.

"So do I," he said, motioning for me to sit in the chair opposite his desk.

"Did you get any sleep last night?" I asked.

"Do you care?"

"Of course I care. Luc," I said, bristling in spite of myself. "I'm your wife."

He snorted and left unsaid the retort: *could have fooled me.*

I didn't know why he felt compelled to continue this Cold War with me. I was more than willing to call for a detente. But *I* wasn't going to suggest it. *He* was the one who'd offended *me*. *He* was the one who needed to apologize or at least make the first move. I straightened my shoulders and sat primly on the chair, determined to be professional if nothing else.

"I heard that Madame Lefèvre's last two romantic encounters died under suspicious circumstances," I said.

Luc made a noise of disgust.

"That's pretty desperate, Jules, trying to throw an old woman under the bus."

"Not if she killed them," I snapped.

"Both deaths were shown to have been naturally caused. Is that it? Is that your news?"

"I just think it's a little incredible that the last *three* men Madame Lefèvre's been with have died suddenly. And my sources said they died under suspicious circumstances."

"Your sources? You mean *les soeurs*?"

His look was uncharacteristically deriding but of course he was correct, so I simply gave him my best haughty look.

"And your own news?" I asked.

He straightened some folders on his desk as if taking his time. Whatever he had to say, it must be really good.

"Are you still determined to act as Thibault's lawyer?" he asked. "Even though you are not qualified?"

Since there was no other way Luc would allow me to hear the evidence he had against Thibault, I could hardly say no.

"I am," I said. "So what news do you have for me?"

"We found a wire among Thibault's personal affects which we believe was used to garrote the victim."

I swallowed hard. Garroting is a vicious and nasty way to die.

"Thibault is a hoarder," I said. "He has all manner of detritus and rubbish in his apartment. It means nothing."

"The wire we found was wiped clean of prints."

Luc tilted his head and drilled me with his gaze as if seriously interested in an answer to his next question.

"Why would Thibault have a wire in his house without his prints on it?" he asked.

My first thought was that it was proof that the wire was planted. The reason I went there first was because Luc's deduction felt correct to me—there was no believable reason for a piece of wire to be at Thibault's apartment without his prints on it. It had to have been deliberately wiped clean. And the only conceivable reason for that was to eliminate traces of guilt.

"It's circumstantial," I said. "In fact, it's less than circumstantial. It's wishful thinking."

"But it is enough to hold him for an extended *authorisation*," he said.

"What was his motive? Thibault barely knew Montrachet!"

"How do you know that?"

"They didn't run in the same circles," I said. "You know yourself that Thibault was involved in the Black Market. Why would he associate with a shop keeper who was his competition?"

"I'm sorry, Jules." Luc began to straighten the files on his desk as if our meeting was over.

"No, you're not!" I said, jutting my chin out. "But this is beneath you, Luc."

"Don't be absurd," he said, growing visibly angry. "I'm not doing this to get back at you."

"Aren't you?"

"We're done here," he said crossing his arms. "You're welcome to talk to your client if you—"

Luc stopped talking mid-sentence. He was looking at something over my shoulder and by the expression on his face, it appeared as if he'd seen a ghost. I turned around to see Davos Bellinort standing in the doorway.

"Bonjour," Davos said, grinning shyly. "There was nobody at the front desk, so I just followed the voices."

A part of me was gratified to see Davos—Luc and I were getting precisely nowhere in our meeting—but seeing him unexpectedly like this made me suddenly note just how handsome he was. Davos had neatly cropped dark hair flecked with premature grey and a strong jawline which to me gave him a quiet charm rather than an overt handsomeness. But make no mistake. He was definitely hot.

Luc stood up.

"Davos!" I said, standing, too. "You're here."

Davos moved into the room to kiss me, and I swear I could feel the very air in Luc's office charge with tension.

"Uh, Luc," I said, avoiding the kiss by turning back to my husband who literally appeared to be baring his teeth at Davos. "You remember Davos Bellinort?"

Instead of moving forward to shake his hand as any self-respecting Frenchman would do, Luc gave Davos a curt nod of his head.

"Please wait in the waiting room, Monsieur Bellinort," Luc said. "Jules will join you momentarily."

I blushed at Luc's rudeness, but Davos seemed to take it in stride. He gave me an apologetic smile and retreated back down the hall.

"There's no cause to be a jerk," I said to Luc.

"Your friend is waiting for you," Luc said, his face hard.

I turned and left his office then, so furious I could barely see straight. I hesitated in the hallway, torn between wanting to talk to Thibault and connecting at least briefly with Davos to apologize for Luc's rudeness. The sounds of shouting from the waiting room made my decision for me and I hurried in that direction.

Elise Lefèvre was standing in the waiting room, her face red with anger. She was pacing back and forth, her hands clenched in tight fists by her sides.

"Thibault Theroux killed Hèlo, and I can prove it!" she shouted as soon as Luc and I walked into the room.

I glanced at Davos who had taken a seat in the room, his eyes wide with surprise at Lefèvre's words. Madame Gabin had returned and she appeared to at least be attempting to placate the enraged woman. Luc pushed past me and when he did, Elise immediately ramped up the intensity of her performance.

"Chief Debray," she said earnestly, her eyes glassy as if she were under the influence of something, "as soon as I heard you had arrested Thibault for Hèlo's murder I knew I had to come forward."

"Good morning, Madame Lefèvre," Luc said. "How can I help you?"

"You can keep that murdering miscreant behind bars where he belongs!" she said, wringing her hands in agitation and looking behind Luc as if afraid Thibault might come bursting out from the back at any time.

"What is your deal?" I said to her with annoyance. "You told me yesterday you thought Marie Fournier killed Hèlo. And now you're accusing Thibault?"

Luc turned to me, his face like thunder.

"Jules, stay out of this," he said.

I didn't know if he was angrier that I dared to speak up or that I'd just admitted I'd questioned Madame Lefèvre without his knowledge. I have to say it's a skill to carry off feeling guilty at the same time you're trying to look affronted. I'm not sure I pulled it off.

"How dare you!?" Elise sputtered to me. "I never said that! You asked me who hated him, and Marie Fournier was the first person I thought of. But she's handicapped so she could not possibly have killed him."

Luc positioned himself between me and Elise.

"Madame Lefèvre," he said calmly. "What makes you say Monsieur Theroux killed Hèlo?"

"Because I heard him threaten to do so!" she said loudly. "Just last week."

"She's lying," I said, hotly.

Elise's face reddened at my accusation.

"How dare you!" she shrieked, her hands balling into fists as if preparing to use them against me. "I loved Hèlo with all my heart. Why would I lie?"

"Of course, we do not think you are lying, Madame Lefèvre," Luc assured her, giving me a scorching look before reaching out to gently guide her out of the waiting room toward his office.

As I watched her walk away, shooting a triumphant glance at me over her shoulder, I was overcome with a matched set of plummeting emotions: discouragement and dejection.

But more than that I couldn't help but feel that I was getting really tired of people telling me that the handicapped baker could not possibly have killed Hèlo Montrachet.

30

After that, there didn't seem much point in sticking around. I'm sure Thibault would have appreciated my coming back to the holding cells to update him on what was going on—and I intended to do that later this morning—but right now I needed to get away from the station and try to sort things out.

Davos and I made our way to Café Provençal down the street as the morning sun spilled onto the cobblestones. We spoke very little until we stepped into the café, greeted by the aroma of freshly baked goods and coffee. A few other villagers were already there chatting quietly over coffee. Davos and I chose a table near the window. Outside, village life went on at an easy pace.

"Good Lord," Davos said with a laugh as he sat down. "What was all that back there?"

"I can't imagine what you must think of us," I said, signaling to the waiter to bring two coffees.

"I think there's always something happening here," he said good-naturedly. "It's one of the reasons I love visiting."

Davos first visited Chabanel last year when he came

down to interview some surviving members of the French Resistance for the Paris French Resistance Museum better known as the *Musée de la Libération de Paris*. Although a lifelong Parisian, Davos has told me on more than one occasion that after the single week he spent in Chabanel last year he now preferred the countryside and village life to the city bustle of his hometown.

I glanced at him as the waiter dropped off two espressos on our table. I have to say, when I think of Resistance fighters, I always picture Davos himself. Not just his passion, which he has in truckloads when it comes to his quest to tell the stories of the unheralded heroes of the last war but also in his commitment to spending months gaining the trust of now fragile elders in order to record their tales of secret missions, and harrowing escapes under Nazi rule. Davos was handsome *and* passionate about what he does. The total package.

"We had a suspicious death this week," I said as I took a sip of my espresso.

"Seriously?" Davos's eyes widened as he gave me an incredulous stare. "Is that what that woman was doing back at the station? Pointing the finger at someone she thought killed the person?"

"Yes. The victim was our village cheese seller and the woman you saw—Madame Lefèvre—was his girlfriend. She was accusing my friend Thibault Theroux who Luc arrested yesterday for the murder."

Davos' eyebrows shot up.

"Your husband arrested your friend? Is he guilty?"

"Not at all. I mean, I'm sure not," I said. "But you can see how it's a bit of a bone of contention between me and Luc."

Davos laughed.

"That's an understatement. Still, it's hard when you are

both so clearly impassioned about your jobs and when personal feelings enter into it."

"That's the truth," I said, feeling my shoulders sag in discouragement. "It's even worse if one of you has no respect for what the other does for a living."

Davos leaned across the table, his voice a soft counterpoint to the clatter of porcelain and murmurs of the other diners around us.

"Look, Jules," he said with a gentle firmness, "sometimes the strongest thing we can do for each other is to forgive and let the tide of love wash away the debris of a quarrel. Yes?"

I know what he said was pretty sappy, but it also sounded true in a weird French Rom-Com sort of way. Bottom line, his words made me feel better. I wasn't sure I was quite ready to act on them—after all, forgiving when you are not in the wrong is *très difficile*—but it was good to at least hear what direction I needed to take when the time came.

31

Luc glanced out the window of his office, his hands balled into fists as he watched Jules walk away with the historian. Madame Lefèvre had decided to take Madame Gabin up on her offer of coffee and a roll in the break room, so Luc was momentarily alone. Regret, helplessness, and jealousy surged through him as he saw Davos put his hand on Jules' back to guide her across the street. Luc felt his muscles quiver in helpless fury as he watched them.

What was he supposed to do? He wanted to believe in Thibault's innocence, but the mounting evidence against him was impossible to ignore. With the murder weapon found in Thibault's place and Madame Lefèvre's testimony that Thibault had threatened the victim, on top of the fact of the ring, how could he possibly justify letting him go?

Just to make Jules happy.

And yet, as Luc thought back to his conversation with Thibault, he couldn't quite shake the belief that Thibault had been genuinely surprised and horrified at the accusations against him.

Luc turned away from the window as Jules and Davos disappeared into the café. He knew his feelings were irrational. He knew that Jules and Davos were just friends, but he couldn't help the twisted feeling he got deep inside his gut when he thought of them together. He imagined that Davos was telling her all the things she wanted to hear: *yes, Thibault is innocent, yes, Luc is being unfair, yes, she is doing important work, no a marriage doesn't require one person to do all the cooking.*

He ran a hand through his hair. He needed to find a way to clear Thibault's name, not just for the sake of justice, but for Jules. He looked down at the evidence on his desk and the ME's report and pinched his lips together as he felt a spasm of despair clutch him. Something wasn't working. Was it his job? Was quitting his only option to saving his pride—not to mention his marriage? Would Jules even want him if he was no longer the chief of police?

He glanced up where he could hear Matteo's voice. The man would be delighted if Luc were to quit.

What are my options? Let an innocent man sit in jail and be tried for a murder I'm pretty sure he didn't do? Why am I sure of that? Because I like Thibault? Because I've had a few beers with him over the years?

He pinched his lips together and felt the beginnings of a headache forming.

Would I let him go—guilty or innocent—just to save my marriage?

The walls of the office seemed to close in on him as he stewed in contemplative silence, a silence that was broken only by the occasional distant murmur of activity outside his door. A sharp knock on the door jolted him abruptly from his brooding reverie. He didn't bother to mask his irritation when Matteo opened the door and peered in.

"What is it?" Luc barked.

Matteo entered, his expression his usual annoying blend of professional concern and urgency.

"Madame Lefèvre decided she didn't need to stick around," he said.

Luc bristled in annoyance. Why did the woman even come? Had she done what she'd intended? To lay her allegation against Thibault and then leave?

"Fine," he said, wondering why Matteo continued to stand in his door at the same time he was wondering how he would tell him he was thinking of letting their only suspect go.

"But now Marie Fournier is in the waiting room," Matteo said.

Luc felt a pulse of dread mixed with excitement.

"About the case?" he asked with a frown.

"She says she saw Thibault at the crime scene two days ago."

Luc had to admit that was odd but not really damning. He was about to say so and to tell Matteo to stop wasting his time.

"She says she saw Thibault there," Matteo repeated. "With Hèlo Montrachet."

32

I glanced around the café and saw that most tables were filled. Mostly they were the elderly as everyone else who had a job to do was out doing it. But it was nice to see the place busy. I dread thinking what would happen if there was ever not enough business to keep it going. The village depended on it. Heck, I depended on it.

Davos and I ordered a basic Provençal lunch of Niçoise salads which Davos insisted on paying for—thank goodness, since I had nothing in my wallet. Janice set down the salads in front of us—bright red tomatoes and perfectly flaked tuna atop a bed of crisp greens with anchovy fillets. She also brought a basket of freshly baked *fougasse*, and a carafe of rosé wine.

After the first glass of wine, I found myself thinking that this was the first time in a month I actually felt relaxed. With his calm manner and simple wisdom, Davos tended to have that effect on me. I was grateful for that. On the other hand, today at least I was keenly aware of his maleness and the fact that—probably because of the fuss the twins and

Luc had made about my maintaining contact with him—he was probably off limits. Davos was all smoky good looks with melting brown eyes and tortoise shell glasses, his tweed jacket stretched across broad shoulders hinting at the strength he'd had developed carrying heavy tomes. Or who knows? Maybe he worked out.

At any rate the more I relaxed, the more it occurred to me that if Davos had been Katrine, I would've spilled my guts about what a pill I thought Luc was being. But of course, Davos was himself a bone of contention between me and Luc and it felt disloyal to badmouth Luc to the object of his jealousy. That was too bad. Because I really needed to unburden myself.

"Is the murder case interfering with your project with the twins?" Davos asked.

I couldn't help but smile. Davos is so committed to his own project of creating the catalog of Resistance fighters for the Paris museum that he's nearly as invested in the success of my project which is essentially the same thing. Unfortunately, me seeing his interest in what I was doing was coming right in the middle of when I felt that Luc was not at all interested in my personal projects.

I couldn't help but think when I was with Davos: *this is what it feels like to be with someone who supports your passions instead of complaining about them or feeling constantly undermined by them*. For the first time it occurred to me that Luc and I might not make it.

"It's going fine," I said, trying to push that unhappy thought aside. "The twins are opening up more each time we talk and I'm getting it all down."

"The committee will want details," he said. "Usually, they'd want witnesses too but those are becoming fewer and fewer by the day." His shoulders sagged as he spoke.

Davos had talked in the past about his own personal project of honoring these histories through a bestselling book to inspire future generations. But for now, he was determined to get these quiet heroes the recognition they deserved before it's too late. Already there were only a couple hundred veterans of that war still alive in France.

"They're giving me details but it's like pulling teeth," I said. "Do you French have that saying?"

He laughed.

"Yes. For us it's *tirer les vers du nez*. Literally, it's pulling the worms out of someone's nose."

"Good grief," I said with a grimace. "I'll stick to our dental metaphor."

Davos laughed again.

"But I have to commend you for sticking with it. I know from personal experience how stubborn those two can be."

"It'll be worth it when I can see the French president or some cabinet secretary pin the medals on their dresses in front of the whole village," I said.

"I know it will," he said with a grin. "But back to your problem with your friend Thibault. Is there anything I can do to help?"

I knew that recruiting Davos to help me find evidence to free Thibault would infuriate Luc, but I wasn't sure I should pay attention to that. I also knew that when this was all over Luc would see his behavior as childish. I had to believe he would. But for now, I needed all the help I could get. While it was true that my French language proficiency was no longer terrible, I was still an outsider. And while Davos was not from Chabanel, him being French made him marginally more acceptable to people than being questioned by me.

"Could you talk to some people for me?" I asked.

"Absolutely. Interviewing people is kind of my thing," he said with a grin. "Who do you want me to talk to?"

"There's an old guy named Dagnier Dubois who used to be a good friend of the victim's but had a falling out with him. I've seen him acting suspicious. I know he'll refuse to talk to me because I'm not French and I'm female."

"What do you need me to ask him?"

"Ask him where he was at the time of the murder and why he and the victim were no longer friends."

"Done. Who else?"

"I hate to ask," I said, "but the woman you saw ranting in the police station, Elise Lefèvre."

Davos laughed. "That does sound like a challenge."

"I know, but she strikes me as someone who likes men and you're good-looking and I've already spoken with her."

I knew I blushed when I said he was good-looking, but all Davos did was grin wryly at me.

"What do you need me to ask her?" he asked.

"See if you can get her to recant her assertion that she heard Thibault threaten the victim."

"What if he really did threaten the victim?" he asked.

"Well, there's a difference between idle angry talk and intent. I can live with baseless threats if there is no evidence to back it up. See if you can find out if that's what Elise is really accusing Thibault of."

"Is there anything concrete that the police have against him?"

"The victim was found clutching a ring that has Thibault's fingerprints on it."

Davos looked skeptical.

"Really? How did that happen?"

"I don't know. I haven't talked to Thibault yet."

"Anything else?"

Davos was jotting down notes in the same notebook I'd seen him write in for his Resistance interviews.

"The murder weapon," I said with a sigh. "Luc says it was found in Thibault's apartment."

"Not good," Davos said, still writing. "What are we talking about? A knife?"

"A wire. The victim was garroted."

"You don't see that every day. Any possibility that somebody planted it in Thibault's apartment?"

"I like the way you think," I said with a rueful laugh. "But probably not. I trust Luc and Matteo not to have done it and the fact is, Thibault is a pack rat. His entire apartment is wires and gadgets and pieces of garbage he considers valuable."

"So what makes them think this is the murder weapon?"

"There were no prints found on it."

Davos nodded solemnly. "Not good," he said again.

Clearly, to anybody with a brain, the only reason an innocuous piece of wire would have no fingerprints on it was because it was in fact not innocuous at all.

"So, I'll talk to Dubois and Madame Lefèvre," Davos said closing his notebook. "But this wire sounds like your biggest hurdle."

"You're right," I said, feeling immediately discouraged.

Davos reached across the table and took my hand.

"Cheer up, Jules. Just take it one step at a time. First, you need to get a look at this wire. Then talk to Thibault and see what he has to say. Don't lose hope. You're a long way from done."

I squeezed his hand.

"You're right," I said. "Thanks, Davos. As Thibault's

acting lawyer I should be able to get a look at the wire. The ring, too. Good point."

I turned back to my salad, my mind suddenly buzzing in a much more positive mode. Davos was right. I needed to see the evidence with my own eyes. And to do that, I needed to track down my old friend Detective Matteo.

33

Later after lunch Davos and I parted ways. He had some of his own work to do to get ready for his interviews tomorrow and I had to see Thibault. I made plans with Davos to meet up this evening at *La Fleurette* where he'd be spending the night before traveling on to Aix to interview his octogenarian. I felt better after his words of encouragement but also worse in a way since those words hadn't come from my husband. In any case, after we went our separate ways, I took a moment to clear some of the wine-induced fog from lunch by standing near the village square where I had a good view of the police station.

Chabanel's square was typical of most small French village squares. It was paved with cobblestones and flanked by a mix of rustic stone buildings with an ancient fountain in the middle beside a war memorial, a poignant reminder of the village's sons who'd served and sacrificed. Inscribed on it were all the names of Chabanel's fallen and the dates of both World Wars.

The city hall where Katrine worked was one of the more prominent buildings on the square. In fact, it was probably the most extraordinary building in all of Chabanel with its classic French architecture, tall windows, steeply pitched roof, and a front door framed by small columns. It was easy to spot from a distance too since the French tricolor always flew over its door.

I waited in the square until I saw Luc get in his car and drive away before I approached the station. It was pretty clear that no good would come from another interaction between us. We both needed to cool off and, in the meantime, I needed to see what evidence they had against Thibault. As soon as I saw Luc leave, my heart caught at the sight of him. It's a very strange feeling to see someone you love and to instantly want to hail them, to be with them, but instead, to shrink back into the shadows so they don't see you. It is a sickening feeling and one that I blame Luc for. If we ever got to the point where we can talk rationally about everything we're going through right now, I intend for him to know exactly how he made me feel.

Once I was sure he was gone and wasn't going to double back because he'd forgotten something, I made my way across the street to the station. Madame Gabin looked up at me in surprise from her desk and instantly her face cleared as she figured out that it wasn't a coincidence that I'd come after Luc left. I'd have loved to slap that smug look off her face but forced myself to be content with asking to see Matteo instead.

I didn't have to wait long because Matteo is nothing if not eager to take Luc's job and adopting his role whenever he could was the closest thing to it. He appeared in the doorway of the waiting room practically rubbing his hands with glee. That didn't mean he wanted to help me, of course.

"I'm here," I said as I followed him down the hall to his office, "to see the evidence you have against my client."

"We are completely transparent at the Chabanel *Gendarmerie Nationale*," Matteo said as pompously as it could be said. "We always work professionally with defense counsel."

He was making it sound as if he was a regular character on *Law and Order* when I knew for a fact that misdemeanors and the occasional lost goat were the bulk of the crimes he was called to deal with. He led me past his office to a door which opened to reveal a room slightly larger than a broom closet. He pulled open the heavy wooden door, the hinges creaking loudly, to reveal the evidence room. Dim light filtered into the room from grimy windows as we entered the space. Tall metal shelves lined the walls from floor to ceiling, filled with an assortment of mysterious boxes and containers, including one labeled *décorations de Noël*. An old ledger book lay open on a nearby table.

I coughed as I accidentally sucked in a dust mote. Matteo went to the first shelf. I saw that someone—probably him—had written in a neat hand the words *Montrachet case* on a card that was affixed to the shelf. I strained to see over his shoulder, but he soon turned and handed me a small evidence bag.

"I cannot allow you to take it with you," he said. "It has been confirmed to show the suspect's fingerprints on it. Chain of evidence."

I looked at the little gold ring through the bag. It was smallish, definitely for a woman. It had a single gemstone, something green, maybe jade. What in the world would Thibault have been doing with such a thing? As long as I've known him, he's never dated anyone, and I've never heard him talk about family.

"Okay," I said. "Did you ask him about it?"

"We did," Matteo said. "He refused to answer."

Then he turned and handed me a photograph of what looked like a piece of fourteen-gauge baling wire. The wire was thin yet sturdy, measuring about ten inches from end to end. It had a silvery-grey color and was made of strong but malleable metal that could hold its shape yet be gently manipulated if needed. On each end of the wire were wooden dowels, cut to roughly one inch in length.

I frowned. "What's it used for?" I asked.

"You mean beyond garroting someone?" Matteo asked lightly.

I gave him an unamused look. I was about to ask him what Thibault had said its use was but figured he probably stonewalled them on this question too.

"It appears to be a cheese cutting wire," he said.

"Seriously?"

I squinted at the wire. Had the killer picked it up at Hèlo's shop when he abducted him? What was it doing in Thibault's apartment?

"Is that all?" I asked.

"So far," Matteo said. "We are still gathering DNA of course."

Oh, please. The EMP had thrown all of us back to the days of figuring it out on your own without any forensic help. Matteo knew it and I knew it and I'm pretty sure he knew I knew it.

To me, the cheese cutter or whatever it was looked like any other piece of wire with handles. I thought the prosecution would have trouble trying to present it as the murder weapon. Especially without Thibault's prints on it to incriminate him. The ring was trickier.

"So this is it?" I asked as if to suggest it wasn't much in the way of evidence.

"You know about the threat the suspect was overheard making?" Matteo asked defensively.

"Better known as hearsay," I said loftily. "It won't fly."

Matteo put the baggie containing the ring and the photograph of the wire back in their slots on the shelf and led me out of the room.

"Oh, that's right," he said. "You haven't heard."

I felt a flash of annoyance. I truly hate these games Matteo plays. I hate worse the fact that he makes me play them too if I want to hear what information he's got.

"Heard what?" I asked.

"A witness has recently come forward to say the suspect was seen with the victim at the scene of the murder."

My stomach nearly fell through the floor at his words.

"Are you serious?" I sputtered.

But trust me, Matteo is not a joker.

"Who?" I asked. "Who is this witness?"

"I am not at liberty to—"

"My client has the right to face his accuser!" I shouted.

Technically, it was the state of *France* who was Thibault's accuser, but I could tell by the look on Matteo's face that he wasn't sure of that. He likely would make an effort to find out but for now I had him.

"Marie Fournier has come forward," he said, his face reddening.

"And she said she saw Thibault and Hèlo in the field? At the time of the murder? What was *she* doing there?"

"She was gathering thyme for a *fougasse*," he said, clearly proud of himself for having asked Fournier the same question.

"Okay, so basically what you're saying is that Marie Fournier doesn't have an alibi for the time of the murder," I said.

Matteo didn't have to remonstrate or argue with me because his look said it all, which was a deeply scolding one that said without words that of course Fournier was not a suspect. How could she be?

She is handicapped.

34

In any case, the news wasn't good. And yes, it shows just how desperate I must be if I keep defaulting to the possibility that a woman in a wheelchair could be the killer. After enduring Matteo's admonishing glances, I was led to the back area of the station where the holding cells were and where Thibault was waiting impatiently to talk with me.

"We'll need privacy," I said to Matteo who was of course offended that I thought he needed to be told.

He informed me that we would have thirty minutes and then unlocked the cell so I could enter before he left and closed the hallway door behind him. I turned to look at Thibault who rose from the bench in his cell to greet me. The night had obviously been a long and uncomfortable one. Thibault was a rough looking sort at the best of times but, after a night in a cell with no access to deodorant or shampoo, he looked even more disheveled than usual. His hair was matted against his scalp, his clothes wrinkled and stained.

Thibault and I are not the cheek-kissing kind of

friends and like most French, he doesn't do hugs, but I held out my arms anyway and he didn't seem to mind too much.

"I'm so sorry this is happening to you, Thibault," I said as I sat down on the bench opposite his cot.

Despite his appearance, Thibault seemed to be in good spirits.

"It's only because Luc is jealous," he said with a shrug.

"Well, maybe," I said. "But they do have some stuff."

"The mysterious ring?" He snorted.

"Yeah, what is that?" I asked. "Did they show it to you?"

"They did. I'd never seen it before."

"It's got your fingerprints on it."

"I can't explain how that could be."

"You seriously never saw this ring before?"

"Not to my knowledge."

"What kind of answer is that? Your prints are on it, Thibault. Have you, or haven't you seen it?"

"Maybe?"

I felt a headache forming in my temples.

"Let me put it a different way," I said. "Is it your ring?"

His face cleared. "Absolutely not."

This was still not a good defense. I needed a good explanation for why his prints were on the ring and then why or how it came to be clutched in the hand of a dead man. Or more specifically, the *jury* was going to need a good explanation.

"What about the wire?" I asked. "Did you see that?"

"Now that is definitely mine," he said confidently.

"Okay, good. What is it?'

"I'm not sure. But I'll eventually find a use for it."

I rubbed the back of my neck and felt my jaw begin to ache.

"Why do you have it at all if you don't know what you'll do with it?" I asked.

He cocked his head at me as if to understand me better.

"You have seen my house, Jules. I don't know what half that stuff will be used for. I find something, and I hang onto it until I need it."

"It had no fingerprints on it," I said. "Would you have wiped it for any reason?"

"Wiped a wire?" He gave me an incredulous look.

"Maybe to clean it?" I asked, desperate for an explanation.

"Doesn't sound like me," he said, frowning in thought.

We were getting precisely nowhere.

"Elise Lefèvre claims you threatened Hèlo," I said.

"Entirely possible. He was a *connard*."

"She also says you threatened his life."

He nodded. "Again. Quite possible."

As I had already assumed. Thibault had said something that, in any other situation—if the person hadn't ended up dead—nobody would think twice about it.

"Why did you threaten him?" I asked.

"He refused to pay me for the Banon he'd sent me to find. I procured it for him as per our deal."

I knew that Banon, a cheese wrapped in chestnut leaves, was hard to find before the EMP. It was worth its weight in emeralds now.

"That's all you did was threaten him?"

"No, I took the Banon back of course."

"Was that a tidy operation, your taking the cheese back?"

He frowned.

"Now that you mention it, a shop shelf might have come down in the process," he said.

"A shelf in the cheese shop?" I asked.

"Yes."

I felt my throat constrict as a feeling of discouragement swept over me. Was that the mess Matteo and I saw? Not evidence of an abduction at all but merely an altercation with an unhappy supplier?

"Okay, and finally," I said, "Marie Fournier says she saw you and Hèlo in the pasture at the time of the murder."

"Well, *there's* your murderer!"

"Marie Fournier is wheelchair bound," I said.

He frowned as if he'd forgotten this.

"Well, in any case she's lying," he said.

"Why would she lie?"

"Because she hates me."

"Why?"

He sighed heavily and ran a large hand through his greasy locks.

"It happened years ago," he said.

"What did?"

"In the early days right after the EMP," he said. "She asked me to find a special kind of yeast. At the time, she wasn't selling anything. The only people making money on bread were the people selling it through the black market."

"Go on," I said. I had a strong feeling that Thibault wasn't going to come out of this story smelling like a rose. He'd been very involved in the black market from the beginning of the apocalypse and as far as I knew still was.

"She asked me to find the yeast, and I did."

"Something tells me that's not the end of the story," I said.

"I sold it to someone else," he said with a shrug.

"Someone who paid more?" I asked.

"It's business," he said. "I am not a charity."

"Okay," I said with a sigh. "So to get back at you, do you think Marie Fournier would deliberately lie to the police to implicate you in a murder?"

"One hundred percent."

I felt as if a thousand-pound weight had just settled on my shoulders.

"Where were you during the time of the murder?" I asked.

If he had a decent alibi that would knock Marie Fournier's allegation into a ditch.

"When was it?" he asked.

"Three nights ago, in the old marsh field a half mile northeast of the village."

He frowned as if thinking very hard.

"I can't remember," he said.

"Were you with friends, maybe?" I asked.

"I don't think so. I don't hang out with people a lot."

"So were you alone in your apartment?"

"Most likely."

Just then Matteo opened the door to say that our time was up. I wasn't sure exactly what I'd gotten from Thibault that would help me—or him—but I forced myself to smile at him with assurance.

"Hang in there, Thibault," I said. "You will not be found guilty of a crime you did not commit. Of that I promise you."

"I know, Jules," he said, smiling confidently at me. "Can you do something for me?"

"Yes, of course, anything."

"Bijou is alone at my apartment. Can you run by and put kibble out for her?"

"I can bring her to *La Fleurette* if you want," I said,

although the thought of the three cats already at *La Fleurette* welcoming another cat into their home was not one I could easily imagine.

"No, no," he said. "She is not a friendly creature. Except to me. Just fill her bowl and check her water."

"Okay, Thibault," I said and then we shook hands.

I followed Matteo down the hall and through the waiting room. Before I left, Matteo cleared his throat and I turned to see he was handing me a small package.

"What's this?" I asked.

"It is a copy of the work diary we recovered from Hèlo's shop."

I unwrapped the paper and found a stack of stapled pages.

"I have examined the document myself," Matteo said, "and found nothing to help our case."

Not for the first time, I was amazed at Matteo and his mercurial ways. I don't want to say he didn't have to give me this copy of the notebook—he was definitely bound to make it available to me. But he didn't have to create a separate copy for me.

"Thanks, Matteo," I said. "I appreciate this."

"I am just doing my job," he said briskly before nodding at the door to encourage me to use it.

Once outside, I stood on the front steps of the station, hesitating long enough to feel the sun on my face. Somewhere in the distance I heard children laughing and a dog barking. I couldn't help but wonder why Marie Fournier would go to all the trouble of lying about having seen Thibault and Hèlo together. Getting rid of Thibault wouldn't impact her life in any way. Could she hate him so much that this was just a way to be evil? I didn't know her that well. She was always pretty peevish, and I imagine that probably hadn't improved now that she was confined to a wheelchair.

But would she really go out of her way to implicate Thibault in murder? Motivated just by spite? With no other benefit to her than that?

It didn't make sense. But that's me, always trying to make sense out of the logic of sociopaths.

35

Davos arrived at *La Fleurette* an hour before I did and had made good use of his time ingratiating himself to the twins by chopping wood, feeding the chickens and helping them restock their tinned goods pantry, especially the higher shelves—basically by being their amenable go-fer. I also noticed he was making a concerted effort not to ask them anything about their time in the war, which I know they both appreciated and which I knew was a hardship for Davos. As a result, the atmosphere was relatively tension free—not something I can always count on at *La Fleurette*, especially with Lèa in residence.

By the time we all sat down to dinner, I could see that Davos was so tired he was ready to fall face-first into bed—or his eggplant parmigiana. Even during an apocalypse, things were easier in the city than they were out here in the sticks. Paris—like Aix—has most of its electrical grid back up now and there are way more cars. It's not back to normal by any stretch of the imagination but I know Davos was struck by the differences on his visit with us.

Heck, just chopping wood for his supper would've made that clear to him.

I'd only had a few minutes alone with him before dinner to debrief about his efforts in the village, and that was interrupted by Lèa insisting he wait and tell everyone what he'd found out at dinner. After Justine said grace and we all began passing bowls around the table, Lèa narrowed her eyes at me.

"Have you seen Thibault?" she asked.

"I did," I said, spooning up the parmigiana before slipping a small crust of bread to Cocoa who sat practically between my legs under the table. "He's in good spirits. I stopped by his place to feed his cat."

"His apartment is not restricted?" Davos asked with surprise.

"It is somewhat," I said. "There's not a guard but there's police tape across the door. I couldn't go inside, but I found Bijou outside. Thank goodness it's summer."

"I cannot believe Luc arrested Thibault in the first place," Lèa said, scooping her parmigiana portion onto her plate and eyeing me as if to make it clear that she considered that my fault.

"Well, they have evidence against him," I said before turning to Davos. "Which reminds me, did you find Monsieur Dubois or get a chance to talk to Madame Lefèvre?"

"Yes and no," he said with a sigh. "I did find Monsieur Dubois, but he refused to speak to me."

"That's annoying," I said with a frown. "And Madame Lefèvre?"

"She recognized me from the police station," he said. "And put me solidly on your team. She wouldn't talk to me either."

"Well, I'm not surprised," I said, sighing. But I was still disappointed.

"But it wasn't a total loss," he said. "I went to the *boulangerie*—"

"Davos is the provider of our bread tonight," Justine said, smiling at him. "Thank you again."

"You're welcome, Madame Becque," Davos said before turning back to me. "And while I was there, I saw Marie Fournier. I figured I struck out with the other two, so what could it hurt?"

I was surprised that Fournier would talk with him when the other two wouldn't. Most people in Chabanel were seriously xenophobic, and Fournier was no exception.

"I didn't really *talk* to her," he confessed. "I basically caught her with a bit of an audience."

I turned to the twins.

"Marie Fournier went to the police today to say she saw Thibault with Hèlo at the murder scene," I said.

Justine gasped. "*Vraiment*?"

"So, what did she say?" I asked, turning back to Davos.

"She was ranting about how the cops finally got it right and Thibault was the killer," he said. "And she bragged about how it was her testimony that nailed him."

"Not true," I said.

"She said she'd swear in court it was Thibault she saw with the victim."

"She's lying," Lèa said.

"Of course, she is," I said. "But why? Just to get back at Thibault? Is she that venal?"

Both twins seemed to think the question didn't require an answer.

"Is there even a place on the road where she might maneuver her wheelchair?" Justine asked.

"Now, that's a good question," I said, making a mental note to try to discredit Fournier's testimony by showing it wasn't physically possible for her to have been out there.

"You don't seriously think the baker could have killed him, do you?" Davos asked, looking around the table, his face showing his surprise.

"Well, she's strong enough," I said. "She kneads heavy doughs on a daily basis, so there's little doubt she could drag Hèlo through his shop door. He wasn't that big."

"But she's handicapped," he pointed out to me.

"That's what everyone keeps telling me," I said. "It's the best alibi yet."

"*Chérie*, you must work to be more generous to people," Justine said in admonition. "You are becoming harder the more you work these cases."

"It's probably why Luc threw her out after only a month of marriage," Lèa said pointedly.

I was grinding my teeth when I snapped my head around to address her.

"First of all," I said, "Luc did not throw me out, I walked out. And secondly, it's been two months, nearly three."

"All I know is that you are here and not where you should be, " Lèa said.

I could see that Davos was embarrassed for me. He was spending way more time and attention cutting his parmigiana than it required. I think we all decided to focus on our meal after that—and of course surreptitiously feeding our many pets under the table. I didn't feel like getting into the details of what Thibault and I had discussed—mostly because it was all depressing and none of it moved the needle in a good way.

I was grateful for Davos' help but honestly his contribution was basically a wash since I already knew that Fournier was claiming to have seen Thibault with Hèlo at the murder site. Still, it was nice of him to try.

Just then, a crashing noise from the kitchen sent Cocoa and all three cats racing out from under the table in a panic and made the rest of us jump in our seats. Although we were all laughing about it seconds later—a copper pot had fallen from its hook—I honestly couldn't help but feel as if it was some sort of ominous thunderclap from the universe.

36

After dinner, Davos and I did the dishes and then we stepped out into the garden with Cocoa. Because it was summer, it stayed light until well past nine o'clock.

The polar opposite of my own pitiful gardening attempt at Luc's place, the garden at *La Fleurette* was well-tended and tidy, a veritable patchwork of lush greenery, organized into neat rows and sections. Justine had created—with Thibault's help—raised beds filled with rich, dark soil and an array of vegetables: staked red tomatoes, leafy greens, and carrots and radishes. The garden paths were mulched with straw and lined with stones so the twins could easily walk through the plot to tend and harvest. When I look at this garden, I can actually understand how the idea of gardening can bring you peace. What else can feed your soul at the same time it fills your stomach?

"I'm sorry I wasn't much help today," Davos said as he tossed a pebble into a massive lavender bush to watch Cocoa ponce on it.

"Don't be silly," I said. "It's not your job to do anything at all. I appreciated the effort."

He turned to face me.

"I'm happy to make even more of an effort if you'll let me."

Hesitantly, he lifted a hand to my cheek. Instantly, I froze. The calloused pads of his fingertips grazed my skin, sending shivers down my spine. The last thing I wanted to do was lose his friendship, not when everything else in my life was so uncertain. Davos seemed to sense my reluctance and pulled his hand back. I saw the disappointment flash across his face before he could mask it with a small smile.

"I'm sorry," he said softly. "I shouldn't have done that."

I shook my head, knowing that I had to speak up before things became even more awkward between us.

"Look, it's okay," I said, forcing a smile. "I just...I mean, it's a strange time for me right now."

He flushed red and tried to laugh it off.

"And the last thing you need as a married woman is some insensitive dolt making a pass at you. I don't know what came over me."

I could kick myself for not seeing sooner that he was interested in me in that way. This was partly my fault for being so oblivious.

"Must be the wine," he joked. "Which reminds me, I don't think I corked the bottle from dinner. I'd better do that if we want it to be drinkable tomorrow night."

"Oh, good idea," I said as he turned and hurried back to the house.

I watched him go and my stomach literally roiled with embarrassment and dread at the situation that had been created between us. But it wasn't that cut and dried. There was something else at play, too. The moment Davos leaned in for the kiss I suddenly realized how vulnerable I was because of whatever was happening between me and Luc. I recognized that I felt this terrific longing to be held and loved and also to be accepted for who I am. Up until this moment, I think on some level I'd assumed that I wasn't going to be able to get all of those things from one person. But spending time with Davos reminded me that it might actually be possible.

Just maybe not with Luc.

∽

Later, after I came back into the house, I passed Davos in the kitchen, and we made excruciatingly painful small talk before going our separate ways to our bedrooms. The twins had already retired for the night, and I did the few chores that used to be my responsibility when I'd lived here before which were to check that those cats who wanted out were out, and those that didn't, weren't, that the doors and windows were locked and the stove embers either banked or out completely.

I made my way upstairs to my old bedroom with Cocoa and after brushing my teeth and putting on my nightgown, I crawled into bed. Unfortunately, the day had been way too intense for me to fall asleep. And the way it had ended with Davos ensured that my brain was swirling instead of settling down.

I kept seeing Thibault in that jail cell keeping his spirits up and having so much trust and confidence in me that his only request was that I feed his cat since he was sure he'd be free soon. It was now when I was so tired and discouraged when it occurred to me that possibly, just possibly, I'd bitten off more than I could comfortably masticate.

Was Justine right? Was I hardened? And what about Luc? Was he really asking for so much? Was I really ready to give up everything I had with him just so I could stand out in ditches in the middle of the night trying to catch fornicating farmers cheating on their farmer wives?

A sense of heaviness seemed to invade my arms and legs, as if physical weariness were the blood cousin to discouragement. Resigned, I reached over to my nightstand to grab the only book I happened to have here. It was Hèlo's work diary. The first thing I did was go to the last entry which was the day before Hèlo disappeared. He'd indicated he was supposed to meet with someone with the initial H. I circled that with a pen since I didn't know anyone, suspect or witness, with the letter H. From there, I skimmed the book from the last entry to the beginning of the year.

It was a pretty boring recounting of how many wheels of cheese he bought and from whom, a rotating inventory list tracking his stock of brie, camembert, goat cheese and so forth along with notes on what needed to be reordered. At one point I saw he'd circled the words *goat cheese* and written *Ask Katrine* next to it. Before she became our mayor, Katrine had kept goats and sold *chevre* in the weekly market, so I supposed she'd once been one of Hèlo's vendors. But she hadn't done it for at least a year. I made a note to ask her what Hèlo wanted from her. There was also a list of repeat customers and their favorite purchases, a weekly record of deliveries and a notation of any upcoming food festivals in the area.

Hèlo didn't use anyone but himself to run the shop, so there were no personnel issues or staff schedules indicated in the diary. Neither was there any information that I could see about profit margins which I thought interesting.

When sleep still eluded me, I went back over the diary

more slowly—this time, starting at the back and moving toward the front—and it was then that I started seeing the initials *DD* showing up. Sometimes they showed up with angry looking exclamation points next to them, sometimes just underlined—again, looking somewhat aggressive.

I flipped to the back of the book where Hèlo had tucked some loose receipts and it was there that I found a single-page log, most of which involved the mysterious DD again. And it was all debt. Not Hèlo's debt. DD's debt.

I felt a pulse of excitement as I realized that DD had borrowed nearly ten thousand euros from Hèlo and had then apparently defaulted on his repayment schedule in the six months leading up to Hèlo's death.

I sat up in bed and stared at the numbers. DD owed Hèlo a big chunk of money. And he wasn't paying him back. I went again to the calendar portion of the diary and this time when I saw the initials DD, I saw that they were usually for a noon or seven o'clock appointment. These were lunch and dinner meetings.

Was DD a friend?

Suddenly, it hit me. Dagnier Dubois. DD.

Dubois owed money to Hèlo.

My skin tingled at what I'd discovered. It was incredible to me that Matteo had this diary and hadn't discovered this! Matteo had a reputation for skimming the important bits and it looked like that's exactly what he'd done here.

I looked at the last page in the diary after the debt log and saw a note that Hèlo had scrawled: *Bastard has the nerve to say he's not repaying me? Told him in that case secrets would get out.*

I stared at Hèlo's words, and their implications vibrated ominously through me.

37

The next morning, I dressed quickly and hurried downstairs for coffee. I was so excited about what I'd learned the night before that I couldn't wait to lay it in front of Luc this morning. I had Hèlo stating *in his own hand* that he had secrets he was willing to reveal about Dubois which gave Monsieur Dubois a major motive for killing him. I was sure this information would prompt Luc to release Thibault immediately.

The smell of sizzling eggs and baking rolls had drawn Cocoa downstairs a good thirty minutes ahead of me. When I finally got there, I found the twins bustling about making breakfast and Davos seated at the kitchen table, pouring coffee with deliberately focused movements. Our eyes met fleetingly as I sat down across from him.

"Good morning, all," I said.

The twins acknowledged me, and Justine put a full mug of hot coffee in front of me. After that, an uncomfortable silence fell as cutlery clinked against plates. Davos stared into his mug and then said softly.

"Again," he murmured, "apologies for last night. Overstepped my bounds."

"What's that?" Lèa asked, frowning at us. "Did something happen?"

"Nothing happened," I said to her and then smiled at Davos. "Nothing at all. But I've got to run into the village. I found a major clue last night that I need to lay in front of Luc."

"Invite him to dinner tonight," Justine said cheerfully. "We haven't seen him in ages."

"Okay, sure," I said, knowing that wasn't going to happen.

"I'm happy to help in any way I can," Davos said.

"Thanks but I've got it," I said as cheerfully as I could.

I knew Davos wanted to help and that he was feeling awkward about the kiss attempt last night, but regardless of that, I also knew his presence in town would just make things harder if Luc were to see him. And while I wasn't going to invite Luc to dinner, I did want him openminded when I told him what I'd discovered.

∽

Luc squinted into the sunlight as he drove down the road from his cottage to the village. Driving these days was the worst, he thought.

When he was behind the wheel, there was nothing to distract his thoughts from her. There were no cars, no bicycles, no pedestrians, no livestock even. He'd had to drink a good half bottle of wine last night just to drop off to sleep, in spite of how tired he was. And the mixture of depression and bewilderment combined with the anger that was with him nearly all the time meant that half the time he didn't know if he was coming or going.

He found himself having to force himself to stop thinking of her entirely just to be able to function. He knew the challenge was to think of her not as his possession or his wife but as the amazing, spunky, fascinating woman he'd known before he married her. As her own person with her own ideas and inclinations.

Unfortunately, he believed he had a viable suspect in custody to a major case. Would he compromise his ethics just to please Jules? Why would she want him to do that? Was it really love if she could ask that of him?

None of what he had against Thibault was enough to make a murder charge hold up. Jules was right about that. It was all circumstantial. Plus, neither of the two women who'd come to testify against Thibault was particularly credible. In fact, in each case it was one person's word against another.

Was Thibault suspicious? Of course. Would Luc need to keep an eye on him after he released him and continue to look for evidence that might strengthen his case against him? Absolutely.

He drove the familiar curve leading to the village, the morning sun casting a soft glow onto the stone cottages that lined the roadway each with their cheerfully blooming window boxes. As he approached the village center, his gaze instinctively went to the police station. There, parked out front, was Thibault's vintage blue 2CV. The car's rounded frame and cheerful color stood out against the austere brick backdrop of the station. It sat in the dappled shade of an old chestnut tree as if it were a regular fixture in the daily life of the village.

Immediately, Luc felt his heart speed up at the thought

of seeing Jules. He reminded himself that she was only there to see Thibault. Would she be angry this morning? Would she listen to what he had to say?

Did it matter? In the end, he was giving her what she wanted—Thibault's release. For that, she might soften enough to be amenable to talking with him. They had a lot to talk about.

Even he knew that.

38

Because I hadn't seen his car out front, I knew Luc wasn't in the office yet, so I made myself at home in the waiting room under Madame Gabin's watchful and malevolent eye. An old pot-bellied stove sat in the corner. In winter, its metal chimney emitted occasional puffs of smoke and usually did little to warm the place. In summer, it collected dust and grime since Madame G didn't consider housekeeping a part of her employment duties.

Thankfully, Luc came in without my having to wait too long. As soon as he did, I instantly knew that something had changed.

For one thing, he gave me eye contact and greeted me. It wasn't a kiss or even a smile, but neither was it a snarl. He said good morning to Madame Gabin and then gestured for me to follow him into his office. It took everything I had not to smile smugly at Madame G who I'm sure was hoping that Luc would have his coffee and read the paper before seeing me.

I followed him, near to bursting with my information that I couldn't wait to share with him.

"You will want to see your client, I suppose?" he said.

Because his back was turned to me, I couldn't tell if he was being sarcastic or not.

"Yes," I said, "but first I need to tell you something that I found in the evidence that Matteo released to me yesterday."

He turned around and looked at me, a slight frown on his face.

"Matteo did *what*?"

"He gave me a copy of the work diary that was found in Hèlo's cheese shop," I said with barely suppressed excitement as I pulled out my by now well-worn sheets and laid them on his desk. I'd taken a marker and circled the significant areas.

"Look here and here," I said, as I pointed to the series of initials in the diary.

"What am I supposed to be seeing?" Luc asked.

"Hèlo met with this DD frequently through the weeks," I said. "Always at either lunch or dinner time. I think DD stands for Dagnier Dubois."

When I didn't get a reaction from him, I turned to the last page of the diary.

"And if you look here, you can see that the mysterious DD owed Hèlo ten thousand euros."

I paused to register his reaction which again, was very little.

"You see that, right?" I asked, beginning to feel a little frustrated that he wasn't seeing this as quite the earth-shattering piece of evidence that I was.

"Ten thousand euros," he said. "I see it."

I should have stopped right then. I should have asked him what was up. I should have realized that for him not to react to ten thousand euros was a hint that he probably wasn't going to react to Hèlo's written threat either. But I'd already started down this road so I turned to the final page where I'd encircled the threat and read out the notation.

"Bastard has the nerve to say he's not repaying me? Told him in that case secrets would get out."

"It's a threat," I said, now feeling annoyed that Luc was making me spell it out for him.

"Yes, I see," he said, opening a desk drawer and fishing out a set of keys.

He got up and led the way back to the cells. I followed him but glanced around as if unsure of what was happening. I was pleased of course if he was about to release Thibault, but I was also flummoxed as to his manner and *why* he was releasing him. Did this mean he believed in Thibault's innocence?

Luc walked to Thibault's cell and unlocked the door. Thibault stood up and looked at me uncertainly.

"You are free to go, Thibault," Luc said.

As Thibault began to gather up his small belongings, I realized immediately that Luc had intended all along to release Thibault today. My presentation of evidence was irrelevant.

"So Thibault is no longer a suspect?" I asked.

"He has not been cleared of wrongdoing," Luc said. "But I don't have enough to hold him."

Thibault stepped out of the cell and gave me a grateful grin. Luc motioned for Thibault to walk on ahead. Then Luc stopped me with a hand on my arm.

"One more thing," he said. "Elise Lefèvre has entered a complaint about your friend Davos Bellinort accosting her in the street."

"Oh, for heaven's sakes," I said. "I'm sure all he did was say 'excuse me, may I have a word?'"

"In any case, I'm giving you a warning that Bellinort has no more business in Chabanel."

I felt my back stiffen.

"You're kicking him out of town? That's harassment," I said.

Luc matched my stiff posture and I saw the cords tense in his neck.

"I am following up on a legitimate complaint," he said.

"I heard that Davos hardly spoke to her," I said. "Old bat."

"Please pass on what I have told you."

I don't know what happened between the moment when Luc was very nearly friendly walking into the office and to this moment, but things were obviously back to being frosty between us. I turned away and headed with Thibault to the waiting room. Luc didn't follow us but went straight to his office and closed the door.

I was confused and thrown off balance by his behavior, but relieved at least to have Thibault free. Once in the waiting room, I stopped to pick up my jacket that I'd left there and when I did, I caught the last part of Madame Gabin's conversation on the phone.

"I heard it from the source," she was saying, "so you can trust me when I say that Madame Lefèvre literally caught them in the act." She looked up to see that I was staring at her. "I have to go, Michelle," she said and then hung up.

I walked over to her.

"What do you want?" she said sourly.

"I'm almost positive you are not supposed to use official police equipment for spreading town gossip," I said.

"That's your word against mine," she said haughtily.

"Not quite," I said, pointing at Thibault. "We both heard you."

Gabin pulled at her dress collar and looked away.

"In fact, now that I think of it," I said, "I specifically remember Luc saying he already had a word with you about this."

"It won't happen again," she murmured, dropping her eyes in a refusal to look me in the eye.

"Come on, Jules," Thibault said, clearly embarrassed by what I was doing.

"Not yet," I said to him before turning back to the receptionist. "Look at me, Madame Gabin."

She raised her eyes to meet mine and the gaze she gave me was not one of a penitent. That was fine. It meant we understood one another.

"Who were you talking about?" I asked.

Her eyes widened and she glanced at Thibault and then back to me as she quickly sized up the situation.

I'll keep quiet if you tell me what it was you just found out.

A look of near respect came over her face along with a slight smile.

"That was Michelle Debris," she said, straightening her shoulders as if she was about to impart world-changing information. "She heard from Madame Demoins who heard from Madame Remé that Elise Lefèvre walked in on Hèlo with the village market nut seller."

I stared at her.

"Juliette Bombre?" I asked. "When you say *walked in on...*"

She smiled and raised an eyebrow.

"*In flagrante delicto,*" she said wolfishly, just barely managing not to lick her lips when she said it.

39

I was shocked and delighted at the gossip that Gabin had revealed to me. And that is not a typical combination for me. I turned to Thibault and handed him the keys to his car.

"Do you mind going on without me?" I asked. "I have a few more details I need to get from Madame Gabin."

"Is my apartment cleared for use?" he asked, taking the keys.

"If it isn't, come to *La Fleurette*," I said. "We have room for you there."

He leaned over and kissed me on the cheek.

"*Merci*, Jules," he said.

I watched him leave not believing for a minute that any thanks were due me. Honestly, it was because of me he'd been arrested in the first place. As soon as he was gone, I walked back to Madame Gabin and pulled up a chair.

"Okay," I said. "Tell me what you know."

Gabin was torn. On the one hand, the last thing she wanted to do was make me any sort of confidant. On the other, the urge to spill the tea was simply too great.

"*D'accord*," she said. "It seems that Madame Lefèvre had been growing suspicious of Hèlo's late nights at the cheese shop. So, she followed him one evening to Juliette Bombre's house. She waited for thirty minutes and then barged in."

Madame Gabin raised her eyebrows as if to suggest the lewd scenario that Elise had walked in on.

"Michelle told me," Gabin said, "that Juliette told *her* that Madame Lefèvre threatened both her and Hèlo with their very lives."

"Exact words?" I prompted.

Madame Gabin frowned in thought.

"*I will kill you both for this!* Or something to that effect."

"Okay. And then she just left?"

"No. Then she assaulted Hèlo where he lay in the bed by throwing a vase that very nearly hit him."

I had to hand it to Madame Lefèvre. She'd taken a personal betrayal and turned it into regal widowhood while at the same time scheming to take out a few personal enemies.

"I do not blame Madame Lefèvre," Madame Gabin said stoutly. "It must have been devastating to discover Hèlo in this way. A man with whom she had hoped to build a life with only to find he had been unfaithful to her in such a humiliating way."

"Did you tell the chief this?" I asked.

She looked horrified at the very suggestion. "Of course not. It is only gossip!"

"Right," I said standing up. "But it's only gossip until it's confirmed."

After thanking Madame Gabin and affirming that I would keep her continued use of police equipment to myself, I hurried out the door intending to find and question Juliette Bombre myself. I was very excited about the prospect of being able to discredit Elise Lefèvre's assertion that she'd heard Thibault threaten Hèlo. After all, it had always been a case of he-said-she-said but now the *she* in the equation appeared to have a very big motive for wanting Hèlo dead herself.

∼

I made my way down the main street of Chabanel with more bounce in my step than I'd had in a long time. It was a warm summer day, and the sun was bright overhead. And I had a possible lead in the case. As I walked past ancient stone townhouses that lined each side of the street, I couldn't help but take in the beauty of the brightly colored doors and the flower-filled window boxes.

I knew where Juliette lived because I'd had a run-in or two of my own with her in the last couple of years. She sells nuts and herbs at the Sunday produce market and dresses like she thinks she's still twenty-five. Now, she's pretty, I'll give her that. But she's also overly flirty and tries a little too hard. And like a lot of pretty, flirty women, she doesn't really get along with other women.

I stopped in front of a pale yellow house with a blue door. A cluster of hanging baskets of petunias gave a pop of color to the front porch. Just then, the door opened to reveal Juliette Bombre herself. A plump woman in her forties, Juliette had curly dark hair and sexy tendrils framing her face. Today she wore a flowing sundress printed with bright lavender blooms. At the sight of me, her rosy cheeks grew even redder.

"Now is really not a good time," she said coldly.

"Oh, no?" I said, deliberately peering past her into her house. "Got anybody in there?"

"Don't be provocative," she said.

"No, I'll leave that to you," I said, edging my way inside.

The interior of her place was as cheery as the outside, decorated in shades of yellow with floral pillows and carpeting. Without waiting for an invitation, I took a spot on the sitting room sofa amongst a veritable mountain of embroidered pillows. From where I sat, I could see an iron pot was bubbling away on a wood-burning stove filling the air with the scent of vegetables and broth.

I have to say it's hard to see the town sleaze as a homebody. It was an image that I found hard to reconcile. I guess I like people to stay in their lanes. If you're the village slut, then wear skimpy clothes and heavy makeup and let people know who you are. If you're Martha Stewart, wear that hand-knitted cardigan and keep a homemade layer cake on the kitchen counter. Mixing the two was a little mind-bending.

"Okay," I said, "so I heard that you and Hèlo were caught in the act by Elise Lefèvre and she threatened both of you. True?"

Juliette walked over to the stove to give her bubbling soup a stir. I noticed she wasn't wearing shoes. The door to her bedroom was ajar and for a moment I wondered if there was someone in there.

"She said she'd make us both pay," she said.

"Those were her words?" I asked. "*I'll make you both pay*?"

"Something to that effect."

"But you heard it as a definite threat to both of you?"

"Absolutely."

"Do you think she killed Hèlo?"

"Who else?"

I chewed a lip and thought about this. I suppose it was

possible that Lefèvre was passionate enough to kill her lover if he betrayed her. I would have thought she was all talk—and most of that whining. But as motives went, it *was* sort of a classic.

"It just seems like a lot of effort," I said.

"What do you mean by that?"

"Well, I mean, Hèlo was the chubby cheese seller. Would you kill in a jealous rage over him?"

For a brief moment, a smile skittered across Juliette's lips as I imagined her trying to envision being so crazy about Hèlo that she wanted to kill him if he was untrue to her.

"Well, we're all different, aren't we?" she said. "I think he was Elise's whole world."

"Unlike you," I pointed out.

"That's right," she said, turning to me, her eyes suddenly hard. "With me, it was just fun. Nothing serious. Kind of like whatever's going on with your husband and Mèmè LaDonc."

At first, I didn't understand her words, so they didn't process. I just stared at her and re-ran the sentence in my brain until I was fairly certain Juliette was intimating that Luc was sleeping with Mèmè LaDonc. If it had been any other time in my life, I would have laughed in her face.

As it was, I wasn't laughing. In fact, my stomach felt as if I'd swallowed a cannon ball.

"Are you okay, Madame DeBray?" Juliette asked with a smile. "You look a little pale."

"I'm fine," I said, forcing myself to push the taunting expression and words out of my mind.

"So it wasn't serious with you and Hèlo," I said, trying to recapture the thread of what I'd been saying. "But it *was* serious with Elise?"

"I guess she thought so." She shrugged. "On the other

hand, Elise is hard to read, you know? She's making a big show of being devastated by Hèlo's death, but I talked to her sister when she bought some nuts from me last Sunday and all she could talk about was the big insurance policy Elise had taken out on Hèlo."

40

As I walked away from Juliette's house, I honestly didn't know which bombshell felt more earth-shattering—the fact that Elise had taken out an insurance policy on the victim, or that Luc might be playing around behind my back with Mèmè LaDonc.

Was that the reason we were fighting? Was he feeling guilty over an affair? Was he sorry we'd married and wishing he was free again? Was it serious between him and Mèmè?

I looked around the street. For one mad moment I thought I might actually throw up.

It was at this point that I started to feel the narrow lanes and stone walls of the village begin to close in around me. I took in a breath to fill my lungs, but it didn't help. The feeling of gut-churning devastation persisted.

I tried to focus on the other bombshell that Bombre had dropped—the one about Elise and the insurance policy. I needed to get a hold of Matteo to see if he could check to see if it was true. In fact, I was already turning back in the direction of the police station when I knew I couldn't do it. My quickening breaths became more and more shallow as the surrounding rooftops continued to lean in too close on all sides.

I needed to get away, to find the horizon again.

I hurried down the street, passing shops and homes that seemed to peer out at me like prying eyes. When I turned the last corner before the town's end, a gust of wind greeted me like a cold slap. But it didn't help. It wasn't enough. I felt sweat form on my top lip as I quickened my pace, each step taking me further out of town and the fog of claustrophobia that threatened to swallow me up. By the time pastureland had unfurled into view, wide open fields rolling into the distance, I knew this was what I needed.

The sight of all that land lifted my spirits immediately. I left the highway—long unused since the EMP—and headed into the first field I came to, following a worn bike path in the tall grass, breathing deeply, and each breath slowly bringing me back to myself. As my strides ate up the earth, I felt the claustrophobic panic I'd felt outside Juliette Bombre's house start to dissipate. I walked until I came to a small grassy knoll and then stopped. Something prickled at the back of my brain as I looked around until I realized where I was.

The crime scene.

The land all around me stretched out bleak and barren under a shroud of gray clouds. Tall wet grass waved limply in the sluggish breeze. There was not a sheep or cow to be seen grazing the sparse tufts of grass that somehow managed to survive amid thickets of reeds and cattails straining from the primordial muck The ground sucked and pulled at my shoes, threatening to swallow them whole in some spots in the sodden earth. A sudden movement in the grass made me look in time to see an adder gliding near my feet. I stepped away quickly and felt the weight of the lowering sky pressing down on me.

Momentarily forgetting about Luc or Mèmè or Juliette or insurance policies, I glanced around, looking for anything of interest but specifically any cart, bike, horse or wheelchair tracks. But it had rained since the murder and the boggy area had demolished any tracks there might have been. I turned and looked in the direction of Chabanel.

Hèlo had been taken from his shop and transported, either alive or dead, to this field, a good half mile from town. Matteo said that Marie Fournier said she saw Thibault here from where she was on the road. I squinted in the direction of the road, about a hundred feet away. Across all the reeds and cattails, it was barely visible.

Was that believable? But why would Fournier lie? Why would she say she'd seen Thibault and Hèlo here if she hadn't? I didn't buy that she did it just to hurt Thibault. I think it more likely that she did it to cover her own tracks.

I turned back to look at the field. Since there was no chance of finding any evidence from the actual murder, I tried to see what there was about this place that made it desirable for the murderer to dump a body here. If it was a woman trying to get rid of the body, maybe this was as far as she could manage? I shook my head and tried to imagine any woman dragging Hèlo's literal deadweight from the road to this spot.

That was the moment when something pinged in my brain. Usually when that happens it's because I'm seeing something I can't make sense of. Something was bothering me about this field. Something obvious, that I couldn't see.

"*Bonjour!*" a voice called out.

I turned and saw a woman standing on the road with her bicycle. She waved to me.

"Do you need help?" she asked.

I instantly recognized Enora Roche—Marie Fournier's ex-partner—and hurried toward her. I always found Enora much friendlier than her partner Marie Fournier. As the gap between us narrowed, however, I noticed the focused set of her jaw.

"Wow," I said, when I reached her and was breathing hard from my sprint across the pasture, "I haven't seen you in a while."

"I'm in a hurry, Madame DeBray," Enora said stiffly, beginning to walk her bike down the road. "If you are not in trouble, I will be on my way."

I glanced at the bike wheel and saw it was flat. She wasn't going to escape me that easily.

"So I heard you and Marie broke up," I said walking beside her.

I have often used in my favor the perception that people have of me as the brash American and today was no exception. It was clear Enora didn't want to chat so I figured I might as well dive right in.

"Yes, that is so," she said with a frown when she realized I was going to accompany her.

"Why?" I asked.

"That is personal."

"Yeah, okay," I said. "Can I ask you how Marie lost the use of her legs? I heard it was a horseback riding—"

"It was not from a horse," Enora said stiffly, stopping and turning to face me.

I bit my lip to keep from speaking. It is always hard for me not to fill up dead space when it occurs in conversation. On the other hand, I have had a lot of experience in waiting people out and having them finally tell me the things I want to know if I can just shut up for a minute. That's what happened now.

Enora sighed heavily.

"She fell from a step ladder in the back room of the *boulangerie*," she said.

"A step ladder?"

"Yes. The doctor said she bruised a rib."

"And for that she's in a wheelchair?"

"Are you really going to walk with me all the way to Parc Sainte-Victoire?" she asked in exasperation.

My eyebrows shot up. Parc Sainte-Victoire was seven miles away.

"I literally have nothing else to do today," I said cheerfully.

"And if I tell you what you want to know? Will you suddenly remember someplace else you need to be?"

"Almost definitely."

"Marie has been having a problem with depression," Enora said, looking down at her hands. "She got in the wheelchair and found…it made her feel better."

A creeping realization began to crawl across my scalp.

"So basically," I said slowly, "you're telling me she's not really handicapped?"

41

Well, that was a horse of a different color as they say.

Marie Fournier had always been my number one suspect. The only thing that had been keeping me from pushing her to Luc as Hèlo's killer was that stupid wheelchair. And now I found out that it was all a sham!

Before we went our separate ways, Enora went to some length to try to convince me that the doctor said Fournier's injury was psychosomatic. I get it. Blah blah blah. She wasn't pretending to be handicapped, she truly felt she needed the wheelchair. Sure, fine. But for me, the bottom line was that first, Fournier was not physically disabled, and second, she was strong enough to have dragged the little cheese seller out of his own shop and kill him.

I walked back to town with a whole different attitude than when I'd walked out an hour before. I was practically brimming with excitement to be able to tell Luc what I'd learned about Fournier. I pushed to the back of my mind the whole thing about Mèmè although of course that would get its day in court.

Just not now. Right now, I needed Luc to see the bigger picture. And that picture included the village baker faking a spinal injury so she could murder the chubby cheese seller in the shop next door.

Just as I turned the last corner and had the police station in my sights, I saw Matteo marching an elderly gentleman down the middle of the street. I was struck by the sight as were several other people on the street because the man was virtually sobbing. Matteo had to practically help him walk. What was happening? I don't have a lot of respect for Matteo and wouldn't put it past him to waste his time arresting a jaywalker when he had a murder to solve.

It wasn't until I got closer that I realized Matteo was dragging a weeping Monsieur Dubois into the police station. I felt an instant stab of guilt. Clearly, Luc had been listening to me after all. Except now that I had Marie Fournier in my crosshairs, all I could see was a distraught old man being unjustly treated. I was right behind them when they entered the police station. Matteo threw me an annoyed look when he saw me, but I could see by the determined set of his jaw that he was bent on booking the poor man.

"Matteo, what is happening?" I asked.

"None of your business, Madame Dubray," he said tersely.

Just then Luc appeared.

"Luc," I said. "Why are you arresting this man?"

A look of exasperation tightened on Luc's face.

"I don't think I need to explain every arrest I make," he said.

I had a sick, sinking feeling that Luc had let Thibault go because I'd convinced him to turn his attention to Monsieur Dubois instead. I looked at the older gentleman who was being escorted down the hall to the holding cells, his shoulders shaking with his sobs. There was no way this frail old dude could have wrestled Hèlo out of his shop door and dragged him to a field. None. Zero chance. If I'd gotten a better look at him that first day when he was watching the cheese shop, I'd have realized that Dubois could hardly be a candidate for Hèlo's murder—I don't care how much money he owed Hèlo.

"Luc, this is a mistake," I said, my hands fluttering helplessly as Matteo dragged Monsieur Dubois to the back.

"Are you serious?" Luc said testily to me. "It was you who laid the case against him."

"I never did!" I said. "I only suggested you consider his motive. I found no real evidence against Monsieur Dubois! I never said he killed Hèlo Montrachet. You've just humiliated him by parading him through town so now the whole village thinks he did it."

"I have no idea how to make you happy," Luc said, slapping his hands against his thighs in frustration. "I've released your friend. What more do you want from me?"

"Maybe for you to do your job?" I said, raising my voice.

I knew saying this in front of Madame Gabin was a bad move, but I was so angry only a part of my brain was working on all cylinders. And not the good cylinders.

"Luc, listen to me," I said. "I just got some new information that you need to consider before you charge anybody else."

"I've had enough of this nonsense," Luc said angrily.

He turned to go but I was too far gone by then to allow it. I grabbed his arm and spun him back around to face me.

"You will hear my evidence," I shouted. "You will not let your prejudice and...and arrogance be the reason another innocent person spends another night in jail!"

I'd gone too far. I knew it. I saw it. And I couldn't help it or stop it. On top of all that, I'm not sure why I thought *this* was the best time to bring up Mèmè LaDonc.

"And I know all about you and Mèmè LaDonc," I said, my hands on my hips.

I could literally hear Madame Gabin scrape her chair closer to be able to hear better. If we still had cellphones, she'd be live streaming the whole fight on Facebook.

"I have no idea what you're talking about," Luc said, his guilty face a stark betrayal to his words. He wouldn't look at me.

"Wow. And lying on top of it?" I said, feeling vindictive and victorious in the midst of feeling like absolute crap.

"I will not apologize for a fleeting moment when someone made me feel good about myself," he said.

"Said every cheating husband ever!" I shouted.

In my mind, this was the part where Luc needed to apologize. On his knees would be a good start. I am almost positive I would've forgiven him. But he didn't and so I didn't.

"Fine," I said, blinking back tears. "In that case, we're done."

"What is that supposed to mean?" he said, his face red with frustration.

"It means I want an annulment."

42

I don't remember the walk back to *La Fleurette*. I think I was so intent on not replaying the terrible argument and my terrible words to Luc that I ended up blocking out every thought or feeling that might try to sneak into my head. I didn't see the trees, the road, the bushes, the sky, nothing.

It's a wonder I noticed the turn onto the driveway leading to *La Fleurette*. Cocoa met me halfway. Maybe she was barking and that's what subconsciously prompted me to turn. I don't know. Because I didn't hear her.

When I got home, I went straight upstairs to shower and change clothes. I have this thing that when something terrible happens, I do what I can to change my immediate environment, like that might change or at least diminish the terrible thing that happened. It almost never works or maybe it works so minimally that it just feels like that. And yet I continue to do it.

When I came downstairs, I was surprised to see what a well-oiled machine the threesome of *les soeurs* and Davos seemed to be. Davos was slicing tomatoes in the kitchen while Lèa was decanting a bottle of red wine and Justine was setting the table. She looked up at me as I came into the kitchen.

"What has happened?" Justine asked.

"So much," I said, giving Davos a weak smile and collapsing onto one of the kitchen chairs.

Instantly Tiny Tim, the nice cat, jumped onto my lap and began purring. I swear your family knows exactly what you need when you've had a bad day.

"I don't understand," Lèa said. "We heard that Thibault was released."

"That's good news, isn't it?" Davos asked as he handed me the glass of wine that Lèa had just poured.

"Yes," I said wearily. "But it only happened because Luc decided he had better evidence against poor old Monsieur Dubois."

"Is that the guy I tried to interview?" Davos asked. "Big tall guy? Looks like he dresses out of a second-hand shop?"

"He's a widower," I said. "So I guess he doesn't pay much attention to his appearance or his clothes. Yes, that's him."

"Luc arrested him?" Justine asked. "Surely he had good reasons?"

"Well," I said uncomfortably, "I found some evidence against him in Hèlo's work diary."

"What did it say?" Davos asked.

"There was a notation by Hèlo threatening to ruin Dubois," I said.

"*Serieux*?" Justine said, aghast.

"It seemed that Monsieur Dubois borrowed a bunch of money and then refused to pay it back."

"Perhaps Luc has finally arrested the right man then, *chérie*," Justine said.

"Maybe, but I also found out that Madame Lefèvre had taken out a life insurance policy on Hèlo."

Lèa was nodding her head as if none of this surprised her one bit.

"And if that wasn't enough, I also found out that Marie Fournier is not really confined to a wheelchair."

I could tell all three of them were as astonished as I had been.

"I ran into Enora Roche," I said. "She said the doctor thinks it's psychosomatic. But there's nothing physically wrong with Marie's legs. She's definitely still a suspect. In fact, I'd say given her motivation, she's a prime suspect."

"*Chérie*," Justine said, "even if her legs are healthy, her mind still has her confined to a wheelchair."

"But physically she is able to get out of the wheelchair," I pressed. "That's the whole point."

"No," Lèa said sharply, "the whole point is that she is *not* able to get out of the wheelchair. Her mental disability prevents it."

I nodded to save my breath because of course I understood what they were saying but I couldn't rule her out now that I knew that the wheelchair—technically—wasn't a real impasse to her killing the cheese seller.

"What did Luc say when you told him about Fournier?" Davos asked.

"I never got around to telling him," I said.

"That would have been important information for him to have, *chérie*."

"Yes, well, it would have, but at the time I thought I had bigger fish to fry. Juliette Bombre said she heard that he was hanging around with Mèmè LaDonc."

Both twins sucked in gasps that sounded like two malfunctioning vacuum cleaners. Honestly, you'd think with everything they'd endured during the war that salacious gossip wouldn't have quite the cache as it does for the rest of us, but they were truly scandalized.

"You spoke with Madame Bombre?" Justine asked, her hand over her mouth, her eyes wide.

"I did," I said. "That's how I heard that Madame Lefèvre threatened both Juliette and Hèlo with their lives—"

"As you might imagine," Lèa said approvingly.

"—and that Madame Lefèvre bought the life insurance policy on Hèlo."

"Juliette Bombre is the one who told you about Mèmè LaDonc and Luc?" Justine asked with a raised eyebrow.

I nodded. "And before you tell me she's not credible, I confronted Luc with what she said, and he admitted it."

"*Le bâtard!*" Lèa said, shaking her napkin like she wanted to kill it.

"So you fought with Luc," Justine said quietly.

"We had words, yeah," I said.

Bad words. Can't-come-back-from it words.

I didn't want to get into specifics with them. I'd done a fairly good job for the thirty-minute walk home of not getting into specifics in my own head. The bottom line was that it was over. My marriage was over. Luc and I were over. I needed some time to get used to that idea before I had the strength to present it to *les soeurs*.

"How do you know Dubois *didn't* do it?" Davos asked—probably more to change the subject than anything else.

"I don't," I said. "I just know Luc's track record. I intend to talk to Monsieur Dubois tomorrow."

"Anything I can do?"

"I appreciate the offer. But honestly, at the moment you're kind of a red flag to Luc and there's already enough setting him off."

43

After dinner, Davos and I did the dishes in a companionable silence. There was still a little remnant awkwardness between us because of the near-kiss last night, but less and less the longer he stayed around.

I could tell by the way the twins talked about him when he went out to get more wood for the stove that they had some hope that he might stay on in Chabanel. But they were conflicted. Lèa particularly was always two steps ahead of everyone else. If she thought Luc and I were having trouble, the last thing she'd want was someone like Davos around to complicate—or exacerbate—things.

"If you're sure you don't need me tomorrow," Davos said as he handed me a clean dish to dry, "I thought I'd head on to the coast before going to Aix. There's a woman there who helped shelter downed allied pilots."

On the face of it, that might not sound like much, but I'd learned from Davos that even offering the enemy a place to sleep in a barn would have been a death sentence if she'd been discovered doing it.

"She's in her nineties now," Davos said. "And in a nursing home so I need to move quickly." He turned to the twins. "I can't thank you enough for your hospitality."

I was pleased to see *les soeurs*—especially Lea who'd made such a stink about having to put him up—go out of their way to tell Davos how much they'd enjoyed his company. Sometimes we don't know what's good for us until it's forced down our throats. I should embroider that on a pillow. It would be a good personal motto for me.

A few minutes later, as Davos and I stepped out into the garden to pick some flowers for the sitting room, he told me he'd had a couple of good conversations with the twins today where they'd actually told him they'd be agreeable to talking about their experiences with him if he was still interested.

"I hope you know what an honor that is," I said. "But I've got them covered. I would appreciate you going over the stuff I get from them though. You can help me word it to make sure they get the recognition they deserve."

He cut several stalks of yellow broom flowers which he then handed to me so I could put them in the basket I carried.

"I promise you don't need my help for that," he said. "Those two are a national treasure. The committee will see that right away. But of course, I'll help in any way I can."

"I'm delighted that they've opened up to you," I said.

"And I'm so sorry if I made things worse with your husband."

"That's all right. It was going the way it was going before you showed up."

"Does he know what he's losing with you?"

"I don't know but I know he's in as much pain as I am. I'm afraid we just can't find our way out of this."

Later, I went out to the stall to check on Roulette. Monsieur Dellaux was visiting his sister in Lyon for a week and needed us to take care of him. Lèa accompanied me to the small shed where we kept him because she wanted to check on her chickens at the same time. I ran my hand over Roulette's coat where he stood in his stall when something occurred to me.

"How long has he been here?" I asked.

"Monsieur Dellaux dropped him off this morning right after you left," Lèa said as she patted his nose.

I opened the stall door and stepped inside to run my hand down Roulette's back hind leg, leaning into him with my hip until he raised his foot. Since he was rarely ridden on the highway or any other hard surfaces, Dellaux kept him unshod. I pulled a few strands of hay from around his frog but otherwise, his foot was clean. I then checked his other feet and turned to Lèa who was watching me with a frown on her face.

"What were you telling me earlier about Monsieur Dellaux complaining that I didn't clean Roulette's feet?" I asked.

"I don't remember exactly, but he wasn't happy."

"I always clean Roulette's feet after a ride."

"Take it up with Monsieur Dellaux. Perhaps you don't do it to his standards."

I stared at her, but my mind was racing in double time. Didn't she tell me that Dellaux had found Roulette wandering about the countryside a few weeks ago?

Could someone else have ridden Roulette?

After that, Lèa wandered back to the house, but I stayed a little longer with Roulette although there was certainly nothing more to learn from him unless he suddenly pulled a Mister Ed on me, which wasn't likely.

I was left with the unassailable belief that someone *had* ridden him without permission. Someone had taken him from Monsieur Dellaux's farm no doubt since there were too many people at *La Fleurette* for him to have been borrowed unnoticed. And besides, Roulette didn't normally live with us.

I used the curry comb to loosen up the dirt and hair on his back, although there was very little. Monsieur Dellaux took good care of his animals. After brushing him down and checking that he had water, I left to go back to the house.

I didn't know if Fournier rode but, if that's how she initially claimed she hurt her spine, presumably she was familiar with horses. Was it possible she borrowed Roulette? Maybe with Hèlo's body slung across her lap? Fournier was a strong woman and could easily have managed it. Well, maybe not *easily*, but it was doable.

On my way back to the house, I passed the gate that led to the road and noticed something white flapping in the evening breeze. Frowning, I walked over to it to see that it was a small, folded note nailed to the gate post. I was astonished that I hadn't seen it before. But it was only because it had now gotten dark, and the note was white that my attention was drawn to it. I unplucked it from the post assuming it was a note to the twins from one of their customers for the blackberry wine they make—truly atrocious stuff but they do have buyers for it.

Curious, I flipped it open while Cocoa and I retraced our steps to the house and read the note. And then promptly stopped in my tracks, my mouth open in shock.

The note read, *Mind your own business. Or people you love will die.*

44

I must have stood there in the moonlight in the garden staring at that note for a solid five minutes. My mind was whirling. The message was clearly intended for me. The handwriting looked vaguely feminine. I had no idea when it might have been put there. The twins were both fairly observant of things happening around *La Fleurette* but they were getting on and Lèa's eyesight wasn't great anymore. I was glad at least that *they* hadn't found it.

I felt horror and fear in equal measure as I reread the note, my brain bombarded with worry and questions tumbling over and over on top of each other. Who would do this? Hèlo's killer? Could Dubois have gotten over here and delivered this note before Matteo arrested him?

Or was it Marie Fournier? Or maybe Elise?

I looked at the house and then down at Cocoa who was cocking her head at me in confusion. This note specifically threatened the twins if I didn't stop investigating Hèlo's murder. I felt relatively safe tonight with Davos here. But he was moving on tomorrow. I needed to fix this before then. I considered tacking up Roulette but decided riding him in the pitch dark was not a good idea. Instead, I put Cocoa in the house—she would at least help raise the alarm if someone tried to get in—and then I hurried around to the front of the house, jamming the note into my pocket before jumping on my bicycle.

I found Luc sitting in the sitting room of his cottage, a book in his lap, an oil lamp burning and the stove as cold and nonfunctional as when I used to live here.

When I used to live here.
So is it truly in the past?

I knocked on the door and then let myself in. Luc reacted, startled, red-rimmed eyes widening at the sight of me coming through the doorway. For a moment we simply stared at each other.

"Luc, I am so sorry," I said.

My words were cut off as he crossed the room in two strides and pulled me into his arms. I literally melted into his familiar warmth, grasping his shirt as if to meld us back together. I felt his breath in my hair.

"Me, too, *chérie*," he whispered.

Neither of us spoke for a long time. Our embrace said all that needed to be said. Regrets, promises, longing. In each other's arms once more, I could finally feel the shadows lifting. After that, and for the first time in what felt like a long time, we talked. We talked without fighting, and without one of us having to win the argument. I told him I was confused and hurt, and that I knew I had been lashing out at him. I apologized for leaving. I told him I knew that wasn't the way to solve our problems.

"You're not the problem," he said.

"Come on, Luc. You hate the way I am."

"No, I don't," he said earnestly. "Truly I don't. I love the way you are. It's just so confusing." He ran a hand through his hair. "I love the way you are," he repeated.

"Just not as your wife," I said softly.

He looked at me as if I'd nailed it, but he still refused to agree.

"I hate myself for thinking it," he said, "but I can't seem to accept you doing the work you do. I hate it. I feel as if it's taking something away from me. I know that's crazy. I've tried to look at it differently." He took in a long breath and let it out. "Half the time I think you're competing with me for my job."

"I'm not," I said.

"I know," he said sadly. "But you're making me look a fool," he said sadly.

"Are you sure it's me doing that?"

He actually laughed.

"A part of my brain understands that I'm the one making everything worse," he said. "But I can't seem to stop blaming you for it. For some reason, I need to believe it's you."

I'd come here tonight to tell him about the note—about the threat to me and the twins and maybe to him, too. But on the bike ride over from *La Fleurette* I'd sorted that if it *was* Dubois who'd left the note, well, he was locked up now and no longer a threat to anyone. And it if was Fournier, well, honestly, there was still the question of how she could possibly have gotten to *La Fleurette* to leave the note in the first place without being seen out of her wheelchair. *La Fleurette* was three miles from Chabanel. And there was no question of her using Roulette since he had been quietly munching hay in his stall at *La Fleurette* the whole day long.

It seemed like showing Luc the note would only upset him with no more shot at an answer than I already had. I'd come because I'd needed his support and love and whether I showed him the note or not, I'd gotten that.

When it finally came time for Luc and I to say goodnight, I knew we had fixed something broken between us, something that had needed our attention. I didn't know where we went from here, but I knew we were no longer adversaries whatever came. Luc didn't try to stop me leaving although I saw the pain and the hurt in his eyes when I stood to take my leave. I hated that but I couldn't stay. I can't put a finger on why, I just knew I couldn't.

I rode my bike down the road until I saw him go back in his cottage. Then I stopped and took in a long breath and turned around and quietly rode in the opposite direction toward Chabanel. One of the things that tonight had reminded me of was, that as helpful as it often is to talk to people, it's probably never going to trump getting into the trenches and getting your hands dirty.

45

Moonlight filtered through the frosted glass windows from where I stood outside Hèlo's cheese shop. Peering in, I could see the light was casting the counter and shelves in a soft blue glow. It occurred to me that my first visit to the cheese shop had hardly been enlightening—especially not with Matteo looking over my shoulder. If he'd found a work diary here, I could only imagine what else there was to find that he'd missed.

I cracked a window and snaked a hand in to turn the lock before easing open the door. As I entered, the door creaked loudly, breaking the stillness of the night, and for a moment I held my breath. Once I was in the shop, the sound of my footsteps echoed loudly. I took a deep breath, the familiar scent of aged cheese and wood filling my senses before making my way through the sales room, navigating around overturned tables and cheese wheels on the floor.

Using my flashlight, I scanned the room. Nothing seemed to have changed since I saw it last. But unless someone had come in and tidied up, I wouldn't have noticed a difference. As I made my way to the back of the shop, I found myself feeling a sense of sadness for the days when this space had been a bustling place of activity and conversation full of customers and laughter.

Now, it was just a hollow shell—worse, it was a vivid reminder of the violence that had taken place here. My mind buzzed as I walked through the space. Had Hèlo been killed here or after he'd been taken from the shop?

I swept the beam of my light across the floor, quickly locating the scuffed marks I'd seen with Matteo. I knew they led to the back door but tracking Hèlo and his abductor's exit was not my goal tonight. I walked to the back of the shop, then turned and saw the narrow set of stairs that led upstairs to Hèlo's private lodging.

My heart beating quickly in the dark, I took the steps two at a time until I was facing a single door at the end of a narrow hallway. Careful not to touch anything, I pushed the door open with my foot.

The bedroom inside was small. There was a single bed, made up with an ancient coverlet, a dresser and a nightstand with a lamp. If what Thibault said was true and Hèlo really did have a pile of money somewhere, it was beyond me to understand why he would choose to live like this.

I stepped inside the room and went immediately to the dresser. Using a tissue I had in my jacket pocket, I opened the drawers one by one and rooted around the worn clothing, mostly under garments. Suddenly, I heard a sound and I froze. I listened intently for several long moments, but the sound didn't repeat. Figuring it must be the natural creaking of an old building, I turned to Hèlo's bed and nightstand. I opened the drawer and found a scattering of pens, a couple of screwdrivers and a packet of condoms.

I reached further into the drawer until my fingers felt a

thick packet which I drew out and shined my light on. It was an old ledger or journal, covered in leather. Excitement coursed through me as I flipped through its worn pages. I scanned the pages but didn't see any entry written after 1945. I felt a twinge of disappointment. This was useless as far as giving me any insight into who might have killed Hèlo. But it might be a good resource for Davos and his research. I slipped the diary into my jacket pocket and stood up to direct my flashlight beam around the room and then promptly screamed and dropped the flashlight.

My heart pounded in double time in my chest. I had been so focused on finding the diary that I hadn't paid any attention to anything else for several minutes. Which was the reason why I didn't hear him enter the building and creep up the stairs until he was there in the doorway shining his own flashlight on me.

"Seriously?" Matteo said.

"You scared me to death!" I breathed shakily as I sat down on Hèlo's bed with a hard thump before getting on my knees to look for my flashlight which had rolled under the bed.

"Explain yourself," he said sternly. "On second thought, don't bother."

I got to my feet, my flashlight in my hands. Discovering that Matteo actually did rounds this late at night was as big a surprise to me as anything I'd learned tonight. He must have seen the light from my flashlight from the street.

"You *know* what I'm doing," I said with annoyance. "I'm trying to find out who killed Hèlo Montrachet."

"We have the suspect for Hèlo's murder in custody! You know we do! It's because of *you* we arrested him!"

"Don't say that!" I said. "Everything you have against

Dubois is circumstantial. You had more damning evidence against Thibault!"

"Are you seriously suggesting we rearrest Theroux?" Matteo asked, throwing his hands up in exasperation. "No, never mind. I don't want to hear it. The Chief's wife or not, I cannot ignore a break-in."

He pulled his handcuffs from his belt and held them out to me.

"I assume you know how these work?" he said.

46

In the end, Matteo very gallantly decided to dispense with the need for the handcuffs and I accompanied him back to the police station unfettered. It was only a little after midnight and I think both of us spent the walk from the cheese shop to the station wondering if one of us should call Luc. By the time we got there, Matteo, at least, had decided to write a report on it and to let me go on my own recognizance.

I'm telling you, I've seen real maturity in growth in this guy in the last year. I still don't like him, but I have to say the old Matteo would've been looking for a place to throw away the key after he tossed me in jail.

It was a warm summer night and since AC was a thing of the past, I think Matteo was looking forward to going back out to wander the village in his version of "rounds," but now that I was here, I had a favor to ask.

"Will you let me speak to your suspect?" I asked.

"Absolutely not," he said.

"What if I told you I was his lawyer?"

"Shall I ask Monsieur Dubois if you are his lawyer?"

I sighed.

"Come on, Matteo. I only want what you want—the right man behind bars."

"We have that man right here."

"So you're judge and jury now?"

"You know what I mean."

"Just let me talk to him. You're welcome to listen in."

He snorted.

"Come on, Matteo, at least you'll be that much closer to the truth."

He frowned but when he glanced in the direction of where the cells were, I knew he'd relent. As we walked back there, I could hear sounds coming to us from the cells and I quickened my steps.

"He's been doing that all day," Matteo said as we rounded the corner.

It was the sound of a man weeping.

"*Allo*, Monsieur Dubois," Matteo said loudly as we approached his cell. "You have a visitor."

Monsieur Dubois was the absolute picture of desolation behind the iron bars of the cell. I hadn't gotten a good look at him the first or last time I'd seen him, but now I could see he was older than I'd realized. His suit was rumpled and stained, and dark shadows had settled under his eyes. His hands gripped the cold metal bars in what looked like white-knuckled desperation.

As I approached, I was struck by the way his head hung low, as if bearing the weight of the world on his shoulders. The air of defeat—and yes, guilt—was palpable around him. He looked at me and then away. He was in every way the embodiment of a broken man.

"Monsieur Dubois," I said as I approached the cell. "My name is Jules DuBray. Will you talk to me, please?"

He shook his head. "What good would it do? Will it bring Hèlo back?"

He fought back a shudder of a sob. I looked at Matteo who merely shrugged and walked away. I put my hands on Monsieur Dubois' hands as they clutched the cell bars. He looked at me, startled.

"I think I can help you, Monsieur Dubois," I said. "Please talk to me."

"Nobody can help me," he said, but his hand moved from the bar to mine, and we held hands.

"Tell me what happened between you and Hèlo," I said. "Why were you no longer friends?"

The tears flowed freely then, and it was all I could do to demand that Matteo let this poor broken man out of his cell. I couldn't imagine this man hurting anyone.

"I always thought we had time to make up," Dubois said, wiping the tears from his face with his free hand.

"Why did you fall out?" I asked gently.

He pulled away from me and turned to face the back wall. For a moment I thought I'd lost him and that he would refuse to answer, but it appeared he was just drawing from some inner resource in order to tell me what I wanted to know.

"I had a friend in Aix," he said. "An old friend who was at risk of losing her house and her possessions. She'd acquired a debt from people who would not be gentle about getting their money. Her son had been badly beaten as a warning and she came to me."

"You borrowed money from Hèlo to help your friend?" I asked.

He nodded miserably.

"She promised she could pay me back a little each month, but she has a gambling addiction. Almost as soon as she paid her creditors what she owed, she was in debt again."

"So she couldn't pay you back and you couldn't pay Hèlo back," I said.

"I told him what had happened, but he didn't care."

"Did you try to pay him back?"

He shook his head.

"At first, I did," he said. "But then my friend fell ill, and she couldn't pay the new loan to the creditors."

"So you started paying *them* the new monthly payments."

"What else could I do? At least Hèlo wasn't threatening to break my legs! I had to do something!"

I wanted to ask him about the threat that Hèlo had written in his work diary, but I wasn't sure the threat had been delivered. If I were Dubois and I knew of the threat, I'd swear I didn't.

"Hèlo must have been very angry," I prompted.

"He was."

"Did he threaten you with anything?"

He looked at me in surprise. I tried to see if there was something else in his eyes, a canny wariness, but his eyes were bleary from his tears, and I couldn't decipher his look.

"No, just the loss of his friendship," he said.

"Where were you when he disappeared?" I asked.

Dubois threw his hands up in despair.

"I live alone," he said. "I was home with no one to vouch for what I say." He looked at me levelly then. "I did not kill my friend. I swear to you I did not."

I decided to try a different tack.

"I understand you refused to speak to Monsieur Bellinort," I said.

He gave me a confused look.

"He is not from Chabanel," I said. "He came here to talk to—"

"You mean the historian?" he asked, and then nodded his head as if he remembered Davos. "I had no answers to the questions he asked."

"Questions like *where you were when Hèlo was killed*?" I asked.

"That's not what he asked me," Dubois said in a flat monotone voice. "Everyone forgets that I am in mourning. Monsieur Bellinort asked how long I'd known Hèlo. I wanted to weep when he asked me that. We knew each other since we were children!"

I thought it an odd question for Davos to ask a murder suspect but then he wasn't an investigator, he was a researcher. On top of that, he was probably trying to win Dubois over. That was something researchers did—try to ingratiate themselves with their subjects—not something most police or investigators would bother with. A twinge of annoyance strummed across my brain. Except, Davos specifically told me at dinner last night that Dubois refused to talk to him. Was he embarrassed that he'd asked Dubois personal questions instead of ones about the murder?

"Hèlo was proud of what his grandfather did in the war," Dubois said. "He was in the Resistance, you know."

I drew my attention back to the man in the cell. I remembered the twins hinting at this. In fact, now that I thought about it, prior to Hèlo going missing I was going to suggest that Davos talk to Hèlo about his family's association with the Resistance. It was a shame he never got the chance to interview Hèlo personally.

"Did Hèlo remember much of what his grandfather did?" I asked.

"Oh, he could recite it chapter and verse," Dubois said

with a tremulous smile. "He dined out regularly on his grandfather's war time exploits. But of course, that all happened before Hèlo was born. He only knew the stories his father told him."

Dubois went to the bench inside the cell and sat down heavily.

"My own grandfather died in a prisoner of war camp during the war," he said.

"I'm sorry," I said.

"My grandfather was a hero to me. Not in the way that Hèlo's grandfather was of course."

"He was still a hero," I said, although of course we both knew that nobody would be interested in writing a book about a man who went off to war and was then murdered or starved to death before being buried in a mass grave. It was a terrible shame, especially since Dubois' grandfather had made the ultimate sacrifice. I didn't know the full story of Hèlo's grandfather but I'm pretty sure he survived the war long enough to come back and father three sons and a daughter.

"Hèlo loved bragging about his grandfather," Dubois said again, looking off into the distance as he remembered his friend and his stories. "He would tell the gas dump story almost as if it was himself who had destroyed the depot."

I looked up, startled.

"Hèlo's grandfather was involved in the sabotage of the German gas depot?" I asked.

Dubois nodded.

"It was very big news in this area. Then and now."

"Wasn't it also the incident that triggered terrible reprisals?" I asked.

"Ah, so you know about it," Dubois said. "I imagine the twins told you. Yes, Hèlo always played that part down of course. And nowadays the younger generation only want to hear about how we fought back in the war. You know, there were several attempts post-war to explain away what the Vichy had done. We weren't all cowards, you know."

One thing I knew after having lived in the area for three years was that, when France came under Nazi occupation, its Vichy government collaborated with the Germans. I also knew that it was a source of deep national shame especially since the Vichy regime's compliance with Nazi policies included the deportation of thousands of French citizens to concentration camps.

"It is so unfair," Dubois said plaintively. "We French fought bravely during the Great War, but nobody remembers that."

"It *isn't* fair," I murmured and then an odd thought occurred to me.

"You said Hèlo told everyone he met about his grandfather's exploits during the war. Did he ever tell his story to anyone outside the village?"

I don't even know why I was asking. I knew Davos hadn't talked to Hèlo because he would've mentioned it to me.

"Yes, of course," Dubois said with a shrug. "He talked to the same fellow who questioned me yesterday. Monsieur Bellinort."

47

I started to walk home, exhausted and confused, my brain buzzing with confusing bits of data and emotions. I realized I needed to stop moving and try to process what I'd learned. I was passing the Café Provençal which had just opened up, so I took a table and signaled to Janice who nodded and disappeared inside to get my coffee.

When Dubois told me that Davos had spoken to Hèlo on one of his earlier visits to the village, I couldn't believe it. Dubois didn't know much more about that interview, only that Davos had indeed questioned Hèlo. Janice brought me my coffee and went to attend to another early guest needing caffeine. As I sat there stirring sugar into my coffee, I felt a surge of emotions swirling through me.

If Davos had interviewed Hèlo, why had he never mentioned it to me? Was it possible he didn't know that the man he interviewed months ago was the same man murdered in the marshy field outside Chabanel? How many cheese sellers does he think a village as small as Chabanel has?

Even if Davos somehow *didn't* know that the Hèlo he interviewed was the same guy murdered in the pasture, that still didn't clear up the issue of why he said he wasn't able to talk to Dubois when he clearly had. The only thing I could think of was that he began to interview him for his book and realized that was not what he was supposed to be doing and instead of backtracking he just decided to say it never happened.

It wasn't great and I would definitely ask him about it, but I could at least understand it. People who are passionate about their work sometimes get tunnel vision to other people's needs.

Once I forced myself to stop thinking of Davos and his weird behavior, my thoughts went to my middle-of-the-night meeting with Luc. It was the first time in a long time that I really felt like there was a glimmer of a chance for us.

"Jules, good morning!"

I looked up to see Katrine striding toward my table. It was very early, and I was surprised to see her. I stood and we kissed cheeks in greeting.

"What are you doing up so early?" I asked. "Surely the girls are still in bed?"

Katrine was wearing a simple *tablier* over cotton slacks and sandals. Even though she was smiling I saw something taut in her expression which reminded me that the last time I'd seen her I thought there might be something going on with her.

"I worked late last night," she said, "so they stayed over at my mother's. It was rather indulgent to have the place all to myself and not to have to worry about making dinner, untangling snarls, the endless bedtime routine."

I suddenly registered how tired Katrine looked. She had

a lot on her plate—raising children alone and doing the job of a full-time mayor.

"Are you okay, Katrine?" I asked.

She looked at me as if she might burst out laughing but instead, she did the most unexpected thing. She put her hands to her face and started crying.

"Katrine!" I said, jumping up to come around to her side of the table. "What's happened? What's going on?"

She tried to dab at her face with a tissue.

"It's nothing," she said.

"Well, it's certainly not nothing."

Just then Janice showed up with a cup of coffee for Katrine and gave me an indicting look as if I'd made Katrine cry. Technically, I guess I had. Once she left, I took Katrine's hand.

"Tell me what's going on," I said.

She shook her head, but she spoke anyway.

"I have been a bad friend to you," she said.

"Well, that's not true," I said. "You've been great. And you've given me work."

"I saw Luc with Mèmè LaDonc here a couple days ago," she said.

I released her hand and sat back in my chair, surprised.

"I should've told you," she said. "I'm sorry."

"I already know," I said. "I found out through Juliette Bombre."

"Now I feel even worse," she said as a tear streaked down one cheek.

"Why didn't you tell me?" I asked.

She looked at me, her face a mask of pain and dismay.

"I think in a way I'm still mad at you," she said.

I wasn't surprised. I mean, I wasn't consciously aware of

it. But now that she said it out loud, it didn't surprise me. There had definitely been something between us.

"I guess I can see that," I said slowly.

"It's not your fault," she said. "It's me. I don't know why I can't get over it."

"I do," I said. "You're busting your butt trying to do everything. If Gaultier weren't in prison, you wouldn't have to do it all on your own."

"I know!" she said in frustration. "But that makes no sense! I know Gaultier was in the wrong. He tried to kill both of us. For heaven's sakes, he's a monster. I don't understand how I can ever think of him fondly."

"The heart is an organ the mind will never fully understand," I said.

Katrine sipped her coffee and looked off into the distance. For a moment, neither of us spoke.

"Forgive me?" she asked softly.

"There is nothing to forgive. I like my friends to be human."

We were quiet again for a moment.

"What's that?" she asked, nodding at the diary I'd found at Hèlo's shop that I'd placed on the table.

"Nothing," I said. "I found it in Hèlo's apartment and was hoping to find a clue in it."

"Matteo told me he found Hèlo's work diary," she said, clearly trying to talk about mundane things to ease the tension between us.

"I know. This isn't that," I said, picking up the diary and flipping it open to show her the childish handwriting inside. "I think it was Hèlo's sister's or maybe his mother's. I don't expect to learn anything from it, but you never know."

"So are we good?" she asked as she pushed her empty coffee cup away.

"Yes, we're better than good," I said. "And Katrine, it's okay to be mad at what life doled out to you. It's even okay to be mad at me. After all, if it wasn't for me—"

"Jules, stop," she said. "If it wasn't for you, Gaultier would've killed me."

"Well, no, he wouldn't," I said. "Because if not for me, you wouldn't have been out on that deserted road in the first place. You came because of me."

"We don't need to rehash this," she said standing up. "During my sane moments I remember he's a monster and that I dodged a bullet."

"Are you going to be okay?" I asked.

"I am," she said with a smile. "And Jules? Don't worry about Luc and Mèmè. You know he's crazy about you."

I smiled at her and nodded, not just because I knew that's what she wanted me to do, but also because on some level, I believed it too.

48

After Katrine left, I ordered another cup of coffee and flipped through Hèlo's diary. After telling Katrine that it belonged to one of his female relatives, I was curious to see if I was right. The date in the front of the book said 1939 so I was definitely holding a piece of history in my hands—probably the reason that Hèlo hung onto it. The name on the diary read *Claudette Montrachet*. I was right that the author of this diary was related to Hèlo.

Claudette had been thirteen and had gotten the diary for her birthday. This really was a special historical document since 1939 the year the war started. Claudette's entries were indicative of a preteen girl in the country in the nineteen thirties. She spoke of her walk to school and of Georges, the boy she liked who raked and baled hay with his father in one of the fields, of her own chores—feeding the chickens, mending fences, weeding, cooking, sewing— and her dreams for her future: a husband, babies and a cottage of her own. It was very sweet and the more I read, the more I felt like I was getting to know Claudette.

Rarely did she mention anything about what was

happening outside her little world. Germany invaded Poland in September of 1939, but that incident did not merit a mention in Claudette's diary. Instead, she wrote for two pages how Georges, the boy in the field, had winked at her.

When her next birthday came in the summer of 1940, Italy had invaded France and Paris was in the hands of the Germans. The event was only mentioned in Claudette's book because the cute boy seemed to have enlisted in the army and she was heartbroken. She spoke of her older brother, Milo, who daily threatened to join the army too, but their parents forbade it. Meanwhile, page after page was taken up with Claudette's heartbreak at Georges' disappearance.

At one point, I put the diary down and realized that Claudette must be Hèlo's great aunt or his grandmother. The rest of the diary in 1940 and into 1941 was mostly a retelling of Claudette's daily quarrels with her mother or a summation of the pen pal correspondence she'd started with her friend Evette who lived in the next village. Whole pages were taken up with descriptions of Claudette's father driving her to the neighboring village in their horse and wagon to get food supplies not available in their own village. Claudette would go with him to visit her friend.

I became so engrossed in the story of Claudette and her daily joys and teenage disappointments that it was with a shock that I turned the page in late 1941 to see a completely different hand had taken over the narrative. Frowning, I flipped back and forth to confirm that this was no longer Claudette writing. It was a definite masculine hand, abrupt and choppy.

Claudette's last entry was November 1941. The next entry by the new hand was dated May 1942. His handwriting was harder to read than Claudette's had been, and I worried why it was that she was no longer writing. It didn't take long before I found out why.

Claudette was murdered in late November.

I read the next passages with mounting horror and heartbreak as the writer—now clearly identified as Claudette's older brother Milo—described what had happened to his beloved little sister. At first, it was hard to follow his sentences or his thought processes. He was clearly overwrought with grief and guilt. He frequently wrote, *"Why her? Why that night?"*

But soon the whole terrible story came tumbling out. Claudette had been visiting her friend Evette in the nearby village. She had begged her father to allow her to spend the night and come back for her. But that night was the night that the German supply depot was attacked by the Resistance. The next morning, Claudette and all of Evette's family along with forty-five other villagers were dragged from their homes to the village square where they were hung.

I placed trembling fingertips to my mouth as I read the terrible sentences before me and put the diary down, the bile in the back of my throat making it hard to swallow. By the time I picked the journal back up again, my hands were shaking. This time I had no trouble hearing Milo's anguish and guilt in his sentences. He wrote that he had been working with the Resistance that fateful night. For him to have revealed this information *in writing* stood as stark testimony to how tortured by guilt he must have been. If the diary fell into the wrong hands he would have been summarily executed.

Suddenly, I felt a jolt of realization.

Milo must be Hèlo's grandfather! The one he was always bragging about to anyone who would listen. The one who'd participated in the depot sabotage. That must mean that Claudette was Hèlo's great aunt.

I felt a terrible sadness as I pressed a hand across the pages of the diary, imagining Hèlo reading these pages and understanding the true cost of what his grandfather and the others had done in the Resistance. I wiped a tear away and was about to close the book when I realized there was one more entry left in it. I'd been sitting here reading for over an hour. The last entry wasn't a written account so much as a list. I realized in shock that it was a list of all the families murdered in the neighboring village of Sainte-Claire-sur-Mer.

I felt tears threaten again. I could imagine Milo going over this list, berating himself, torturing himself for every name on it. He even had the ages listed next to each of the victims.

I forced myself to go down the list until I found the name *Claudette Montrachet, age fifteen*. After a shaky breath, I went down the rest of the list, tears blurring my vision, until I came to a set of five names all the same. A family. I blinked and my tears streaked down my cheeks as I felt a shudder of incomprehension ripple through me.

Bellinort.

I stared at the name, my brain whirling in confusion and mounting dread.

That was Davos' last name.

I looked up, and stared into the distance, my mind whirling in confusion and dread. The village square with its prominent war memorial and city hall down the street was just visible from where I sat. And yet I didn't see it. My mind was racing so fast I was unaware of anything around me. I glanced back down at the diary and at the list of the names of the murdered.

Davos's family is from this area?

I looked around in complete befuddlement. Is it a common name? I'd never heard it before. Surely a historian would know where his people came from. Davos told me he came from Paris. I looked back at the diary.

He lied.

I let out a slow intake of breath at the realization. And its implications. Because as soon as I realized that Davos must have held Hèlo's grandfather accountable for the murder of his family—I realized that he must certainly hold the twins accountable for it too.

49

I pedaled furiously toward *La Fleurette*, the uneven pavement jolting me and threatening to throw me off balance the whole way. My heart hammered against my ribs in a wild, erratic rhythm that mirrored the frantic pace of my thoughts. I could feel the panic and fear driving me forward like a demon on my heels. My breath came in sharp, jagged gasps. The image of Davos, with his friendly face, his unassuming manner, kept morphing into the sinister entity he really was and played on a loop in my brain.

How could I have been so stupid? How could I not have seen him for who he was?

Dread coiled around my spine like a serpent ready to strike, ready to consume me as I neared *La Fleurette*. As I got closer, I leaped off the bike, letting it fall, and sprinted the last stretch towards the front door. My heart pounded in my throat as I realized I didn't hear Cocoa barking a greeting.

I jerked open the unlocked front door and ran inside, with only the sound of my own footsteps echoing through the *mas*.

"No, no, no," I whispered, a mantra against the worst of my fears.

I ran first to the kitchen and then up the stairs to the bedrooms, my mind in constant motion conjuring the horrifying conclusion of what must have happened.

"Justine! Lèa! Cocoa!" I cried out, my voice seeming to crack with the strain of my desperate hope to hear them answer me.

A soft, muted bark came from somewhere nearby.

The cellar!

I raced back to the kitchen and jerked open the door that led to the wine cellar. Cocoa bolted through it, launching into my arms and then scrambling to her feet to race to the front door. She was frantic, her naturally protective instincts having been painfully thwarted by the confinement.

I hurried after her and ran my hands through her coat, taking a moment to be grateful that Davos hadn't hurt her. Even holding her, which usually calms me, I felt my panic begin to ratchet up into a kind of terror that clawed at the edges of reason and sanity. I released her, and she bolted again toward the front door with a frantic energy that mirrored my own fear, my own helplessness.

I forced myself to stay calm and to think rationally. I looked around the kitchen to see if there was any clue at all to where they might have gone. To where Davos might have taken them. I forced myself to go into the garden to make sure they weren't there, and I came back trembling with relief because I was half afraid I would've found their bodies.

I came back inside and attached the leash to Cocoa's collar.

"Come on, girl," I said, my voice raspy. "Let's go find them."

∽

Luc's cottage was only two miles from *La Fleurette* and, riding my bike with Cocoa flying beside me, I made it in minutes. I thanked God when I turned the last bend to his place and saw that his car was still in the drive. It was already mid-morning. I hopped off my bike and dropped the leash.

"Luc! Luc!" I called as I raced to the front porch and tried the door. It was locked.

Within seconds, he opened it. He was dressed for work, a cup of coffee in one hand. But seeing me, his expression quickly changed from delight to dread.

"What has happened?" he asked.

"Luc, it's Davos," I said. "I don't know all the details, but he's taken *les soeurs*. We've got to find them!"

"*Chérie*, come in and—"

"We don't have time for that!" I said, whirling out of his reach.

My mind was spinning as my eyes darted to his car. With it, we could go anywhere to search for them. We could go as far as Aix if we needed to. Even Marseilles. Would Davos have taken them far? How could he? They were all on foot.

"*Chérie*," Luc said patiently. "We need to form a plan. We can't just race around the countryside."

I knew he was right but, like Cocoa, every fiber in my being was telling me to *move*, to act. I felt his hand on my arm. He was tugging me into the cottage.

"Tell me why you think he has taken *les soeurs*," Luc said

reasonably as he pulled me into his cottage. I smelled coffee on the counter. He'd made coffee.

"Because," I said, "it all fits."

He directed me to a chair.

"Tell me how," he said calmly, gently.

I sat down and suddenly felt the exhaustion from my stress and panic cascade over me. Cocoa came to sit at my feet and to look at me as if wondering why we had stopped. But Luc was right. We needed a plan, a direction.

"Davos told me he didn't talk to Dubois," I said. "But he did. He also never mentioned that he'd talked to Hèlo. But he did."

I saw Luc's eyebrows shoot up in surprise.

"He did not tell you? Well, that could mean anything. He might have—"

"No, Luc! I found a diary in Hèlo's apartment—it belonged to Hèlo's great aunt. A great aunt he never met because she was murdered before he was born, before his father was even born."

The look of confusion on Luc's face settled into a mask of mild concern. He turned and poured a cup of coffee and handed it to me without saying a word.

"Hèlo's people—his grandfather," I said, "was responsible for the gas depot sabotage during the war that resulted in fifty people being murdered by the Nazis. Five of those people were relatives of Davos."

"*Mon Dieu*," Luc said. "Do you think Davos killed Hèlo?"

"Think about it," I said. "He interviewed him. He found out that Hèlo was the descendent of the man responsible in his mind for the massacre of so many members of his family. And Davos is plenty strong enough to drag Hèlo from the shop."

Luc sat down, a frown on his face.

"We should have known," I said. "Nobody from around here would bury a body where we found it. Think about it. It's a frigging flood plain! Only someone not from the area would do that!"

As soon as I'd spoken, I wished I could snatch my words back. I didn't look at Luc's face, but I know my words must have been knives straight into his heart. Because if *I* was lambasting myself for not seeing it sooner, then he surely was. But it was too late to tiptoe around his feelings now.

"I disagree," Luc said. "He must have seen it was marshy. There had to be another reason."

"There was," I said as the light went on in my brain. "In the research I did for Katrine, I came across documents that indicated that that field was used as a killing field for some of the reprisals from the Nazis."

"*Vraiment?*"

I could see Luc was shocked. It's hard to envision the place we live as having been a bloody battlefield not so long ago. And most people who would've remembered that time were gone now.

"That's why he chose it to dump Hèlo's body," I said wearily. "It all makes sense. And think about it, Luc. Garroted? That's the execution method the Resistance used on those who betrayed them. Davos knows exactly what he's doing."

Luc stood up. I could see he believed what I was telling him. He had a unassailable look of conviction in his face and in his movements.

"Do you have any idea where he might have taken them?" he asked.

I put my head in my hands.

"I've been trying to think," I said. "But nothing makes sense."

"Think harder, *chérie*," Luc said. "It sounds as if it has less to do with his knowledge of the area than the symbolic justice he craves."

I looked at him then and struggled to see a glimmer of enlightenment peeking through the morass of conflicting clues. I got up to pace the room furiously rubbing my temples as clues and suspicions swirled chaotically in my head. Time was of the essence. I had no doubt Davos intended to kill the twins.

"Maybe he won't choose the location," Luc said. "Maybe he'll make one of the twins choose where he kills them."

Collapsing into a chair, I squeezed my eyes shut and forced my racing thoughts to slow. Breath by breath, I willed each theory to the forefront of my mind to be scrutinized for flaws. Nothing seemed to connect. It was all disjointed incoherent fragments. Then, as if from some great distance, an echo rose through the noise and the pieces slammed together with a mental click that made me shoot to my feet, my eyes flying open in horrible realization.

I looked at Luc as the light bulb broke through the fog of garbled information.

"He wouldn't have to ask them to choose the location," I said. "I know exactly where he's taken them."

50

The large concrete building loomed straight ahead, its bulk faded and crumbling with age. Sand-colored paint had peeled off the corrugated metal siding, revealing rusted steel beneath.

Outside, the encroaching forest threatened to reclaim what was once a hub of military activity. Now, only echoing silence remained within the decaying husk of the old supply depot that stood witness to time continuing its inevitable march. Inside the building, decades of dust and disuse lay thick. Crates and pallets that once held provisions and equipment sat empty, falling apart where they were not already collapsed.

Rotten wooden floors creaked underfoot as Davos herded the two women between the broken machines and tools decaying in the gravel in front of the looming building. A few feet away was a ledge that plummeted in a forty-foot drop to the broken landscape below of corroded artillery pieces and collapsing metal storage sheds.

It was here, Davos thought as he looked around. Here was the reason for the massacre of Sainte-Claire-sur-Mer.

He turned to look at the two sisters and reminded himself that this place was not the reason. People were the reason. *These* people.

"What do you see?" he asked them. "Do you see now what you did? Do you see it?"

"This is madness, Monsieur Bellinort," Justine said to him. "We were as devastated by the reprisals as anyone."

"Did you bury a child?" Davos asked. "Did you mourn a sister killed in her teens?"

Both twins stood, their backs to the decaying machinery around them. For a moment Davos could see them as they'd been. Young and slim, their faces full of passion and vibrancy. Now they just looked tired. It wasn't the same. Not nearly. How does killing two old women atone for children who never got to live their lives? Who never got a chance to fall in love, to marry, to have children of their own?

"Every patriot knew the risks," Lèa was saying, her mouth a determined fierce line.

"Easy for you to say since none of your family paid the price of those risks," Davos spat.

"You are weak," Lèa retorted, her face hard and unafraid. "You would have betrayed your family before the Gestapo asked their first question."

"Lèa, don't," Justine said. She put a hand on Lèa's arm as if to calm her, restrain her.

"Look at him, Justine," Lèa said derisively. "He is a coward."

"Does a coward do this?" Davos said, waving the rope he held in one hand. "Does a coward get justice for his family even seventy years later?"

"Are you sure you are not German?" Lèa asked. "You behave as if you fought for the other side."

"Shut up!" he snarled, his face a flinch of agony and

fury. "My family died for your grandstanding! Do you hear me? My grandparents and great-grandparents died so you could be a hero!"

"I think they died so you could be a free Frenchman," Lèa said, before spitting on the ground between them.

"Did you know that years ago, the children used to come to the marsh where I killed Hèlo to plant flowers for the ones murdered?" Davos said. "But now nobody remembers. It's just a field that won't grow anything. But here? Do you remember it?"

The rolling bay doors behind the twins had once been able to slide open with ease, but now they hung askew off damaged tracks.

"Davos," Justine said, "you know it was not our intention to have anyone from that village get hurt."

"You knew there would be reprisals! You all knew it! *Acceptable collateral damage* circa nineteen forty-three."

"You ask us what we see here," Justine said as she swept a hand at the decrepit machinery all around them. "What I see are the remnants of the tyranny we fought against."

"Sacrificing my family in the process!"

"We all would have gladly died to preserve our freedom," Lèa said. "Even the ones who were executed."

"How do you know? Did anybody ask my thirteen-year-old great aunt? Or my great grandmother? Did anyone ask the five-year-old twins who died?"

Davos stood alone, his whole frame trembling now with the weight of his despair and fury. His tears spilled over and traced wet paths down both cheeks—the very picture of a man on the precipice of surrendering to darker impulses.

He took four strides to where the twins stood and grabbed Justine by the arm, dragging her to the ridge under a broken structure of a wooden watchtower. He lifted a warning finger to Lea.

"Stay where you are, or she dies now instead of later."

Both women stood frozen until Davos turned and threw the long end of the noose over the top beam of the watchtower.

51

Luc and I huddled in the bushes, our eyes trained on the looming remains of the supply depot. I stared at the structure and tried to imagine how it must have looked seventy years ago when it was a bustling supply depository, the hub of the German troop presence for this area. Although we weren't far, a mere twenty yards, I used Luc's binoculars. With them I could see Davos facing the two elderly twins. They were not bound.

It took all the strength I had not to race over there and physically attack Davos.

As we watched, Davos paced back and forth in front of them, his arms gesturing wildly. The twins stood stoically, their eyes locked on him. I couldn't hear what was being said, but the tension in the air was palpable even from this distance. I gripped the binoculars tighter, willing myself to stay hidden and not do anything rash.

Luc's hand landed on my shoulder, grounding me in the present. I turned to look at him. He shook his head, indicating that we should wait for an opportunity to make our move. I couldn't see if Davos had a weapon but if he intended to kill the twins like he did Hèlo, a wire would slip unobtrusively in a pocket.

"What's the plan, Luc?" I whispered hoarsely.

He hesitated. In that pause I saw he had no plan. Worse, he was afraid. Later I'd realize he wasn't afraid for himself but for all the ways this expedition could go very badly wrong for me and Justine and Lèa. But all I knew right then was that he wasn't moving fast enough.

I turned back to the group in front of us and saw Davos pull out a length of rope. My heart caught in my throat. Not a rope. A noose.

"You need to get behind him," I said to Luc.

"But how will that—?"

I didn't hear the rest of that because I was on my feet and crashing through the bushes toward the trio. I leapt over broken machinery, adrenaline pumping through my veins. As I ran, the only sounds I could hear were the crunch of gravel and broken glass underfoot, and the pounding of my heart in my ears. I dodged hulking pieces of rusting ironware, my pathway a maze of disabled jeeps, flattened tires and dented oil drums. My eyes were focused on the three people ahead of me.

Davos was the first to look in my direction. I could see he wasn't surprised. In fact, I'm not sure he didn't give me a knowing smile when he saw me running toward them.

"*Chérie*, no!" Justine cried out.

Davos stood with Justine on the brink of some kind of ledge. He held the rope in one hand and tightened the noose around her neck. At the same time, he held up a hand signaling me to stop. I slowed my steps. He had looped the rope over a thick wooden beam. He pushed Justine to the rim of the ledge.

Seeing Justine standing on the edge of the precipice, it

was all I could do not to scream. Davos was going to push her over the cliff to her death. It might not be the symbolic gesture he was hoping for, but Justine would be just as dead.

I watched Davos as his hands clenched and unclenched in what looked like a futile attempt to grasp the self-control that was slipping through his fingers. He was about to do something terrible. Something he couldn't come back from. Unless someone stopped him.

"So what's the plan, Davos?" I asked, trying to keep my voice steady.

I was only ten feet from him and Justine. Too far to rush him and reach her in time.

"I don't want to hurt you, Jules," he said, continuing to clench his hands. "But they deserve what's coming. You of all people can see that."

"Do you really want me to tell you what I see?" I said.

"Don't goad me, Jules. I don't want to hurt you. But I have to do this."

"You don't," I said. "The sisters did not kill your family."

"Yes, they did! And they've gotten off scot-free all these years! They need to pay!"

This was hopeless. He wasn't able to listen to reason. But maybe there was another way.

"So, tell me," I said. "After you kill them, will you then do the world a favor and kill yourself?"

His face flushed deep crimson.

"How like an American to mock the ultimate sacrifice," he said bitterly.

"Killing old women is what you call the ultimate sacrifice? I guess it must be different for the French. In America we honor our war heroes."

"Don't provoke me! I know you're just trying to upset me! My mind's made up!"

My brain was racing as I watched Justine's face, white with tension and fear. If I were to rush him, all he had to do was give her a shove.

"You need help, Davos," I said, glancing at Lèa.

I saw she was holding something small in her hands, but I couldn't see what it was as she was partially in shadow. Was it a weapon of some kind? I was sure Davos would not have been so stupid as not to check the twins for weapons before dragging them here.

"I'm astonished you feel the need to avenge your family by killing your country's heroes," I said. "If you want revenge, why not go to Berlin and see if there are any German soldiers still alive you can kill?"

"These two knew what would happen!" Davos screamed.

He didn't look like the man I'd just spent two days with over multiple cups of coffee. He looked possessed, like he was fighting a war within himself and losing badly. Those same hands that had reached out to give me reassurance trembled with unnerving energy as a physical manifestation of his inner chaos.

"We did care," Justine said, her voice tremulous. "We just cared about our country's freedom more."

"Your family would've agreed with us," Lèa said. "If they were honorable Frenchmen."

"They were children!" he screeched. "They had no idea why they were dying!"

"We were at war!" Lèa said. "They knew that much."

"No, no!" he said feverishly. "You can't talk your way out of this. They were innocents killed by their own people."

"That's you insisting on seeing it that way," I said, taking a step toward him and Justine. "You know your family wouldn't hold *les soeurs* to blame."

"It doesn't matter what they would do. Vengeance is my responsibility."

"Have you got a mother still alive who might be horrified when she finds out what you've done?" I asked. "How about a brother or sister? Someone whose same last name will now be spread across all media outlets announcing how you died a Nazi-loving traitor?"

"Stop saying that! This has nothing to do with the Nazis!"

"It has everything to do with them," Lèa said with grim determination. "The Nazis murdered your family. And they did worse for less reason. Does this mean you give them a pass for Auschwitz?"

"Yeah, what about the camps?" I said to him. "Who are you blaming for the eight million people murdered there? Charles DeGaulle? Eisenhower?"

"Don't try to twist my logic! I am an historian! Do you think I don't know the facts?"

He was right of course. Trying to talk to him or make him re-set his thinking about what had happened was hopeless. After all, he'd deliberately planned and cold-bloodedly garroted Hèlo Montrachet. He wasn't suddenly going to reconsider everything he believed at this point.

Just then, I saw Luc emerge from the shrubbery just behind Davos. My heart juddered in fear. Luc was unarmed. In the time it would take him to reach Davos, Justine would be sailing over the cliff to her death. I prayed Luc knew to stay hidden and not do anything rash.

I saw Davos was getting more agitated which could only end one way. I didn't know how it would help, but if I could just slow things down, I might find a way out of this for all of us.

"Do you mind telling me how Hèlo was found clutching

a ring with Thibault's prints on it?" I asked, relieved to see Luc disappear from sight although I hoped he had a plan because beyond stalling Davos for time, I was fresh out.

"That was serendipitous," Davos said, the hand holding the noose at Justine's throat relaxing. "I saw Thibault at a flea market in Aix and noticed him pick up a piece of jewelry and then put it back down. After he walked on, I put on gloves, and bought the ring."

"So you were intending to frame Thibault for the murder all along?"

This was a surprise. I didn't know Davos even knew Thibault before this week.

"I wasn't sure what I was going to use it for, exactly. I have a few other items I've collected over the months with various people's DNA on them. I had no other motive or reason for putting that ring in Hèlo's hand beyond wanting to create a misdirection for the police. And boy did it ever."

"Did you worry that Thibault might have an alibi?"

Davos shrugged.

"An alibi can be bought. But DNA is unassailable."

"And the wiped-clean wire you used to kill Hèlo?"

He laughed.

"I threw away the wire I used on him. But as soon as I knew Thibault was being held for Montrachet's murder, I broke into his place and found a wire that was close enough. I wiped it clean. The beauty of it, of course, was that the wire really was his. Pretty genius."

"Quit praising yourself," I said. "You sound pathetic."

"Do I really? Did I sound pathetic when I went looking for you, pretending I'd just come to town two days ago when I'd been here, hiding, for a week? Or do *you* sound pathetic because you never asked how I got to Chabanel? There was no bus from Paris the day you and I met up. You screwed up, Jules."

I absorbed the hit, all the more painful since it was true. Because I trusted him, it never occurred to me to wonder about how he'd arrived in the village at the time he did.

"You borrowed Roulette," I said. "When you killed Hèlo. You broke into Monsieur Dellaux's barn and took him out."

"Well done, Miss Marple," Davos said sarcastically. "I needed to move the body and in case you haven't noticed, I don't have a car."

"And you wrote me the threatening note."

"Now *that* was an act of kindness," he said. "I was trying to avoid this very situation."

"Enough of this!" Lèa shouted.

She held up her hand, now no longer in shadow, and I saw what she held. And when I did, my whole body began to tremble violently.

52

She held a Stielhandgranatel. A World War II German hand grenade.

My mouth went dry as I stared at it in Lèa's trembling elderly arm holding it high in the air.

"I've already pulled the pin," Lèa said, holding up her other hand to show the pin. "I can put it back in or toss this into your arms so you may see your massacred family in person."

I must say I thought that was a bit provocative under the circumstances. And from the look on Davos' face, he appeared to be seriously considering the macabre suggestion. I wasn't all that surprised that Lèa had found an active ordinance—if it was still live. The French were useless at post-war clean up. But right at this moment, I didn't know if I should be glad or terrified.

No, terrified. Definitely terrified.

"Let my sister go, Davos," Lèa said. "You don't have to die."

That was the moment when I began to doubt Lèa's accurate analysis of the situation. Because I think Davos was perfectly fine with the idea of dying. And the idea of going out—all of us together in a bang—might just appeal to his perverted sense of justice.

"But *you* do have to die," Davos said before turning and giving Justine a soft, nearly tender push.

My scream was trapped in my throat as I watched it happen in graceful slow motion. Justine seemed to wobble at first, her eyes wide with disbelief and shock. Then she went over the edge. Her arms reached out desperately to grab at Davos. But he stepped back and there was nothing but space. One moment Justine was there and the next, she was gone, the space next to Davos a throbbing emptiness in my vision. Before I could react, I heard the ominous thump of the hand grenade as it landed at Davos' feet. He startled and then stared at it. In that split second, I saw his mind wrestling with whether he should pick it up and throw it or—

In that fraction of a second of indecision, the world went briefly, brutally silent, as if the very air was holding its breath. And then a sound exploded out of the silence with a deafening roar. A concussive wave of noise ripped through the air, as if were shredding the very atmosphere.

The barrage of noise was followed by a deep, resonant boom that echoed off the surrounding landscape. And then I heard the rest of it—the splintering of wood, the clattering of dislodged stones, the metallic screech of bending steel from the nearby structures as they blew. The shockwave slammed into me and knocked me off my feet. I felt a rush of heated wind whip past me, carrying with it an abrasive sting of rubbish and flying dirt that razored my skin like a sandblaster.

I lay on the ground, disoriented, my ears ringing. Dust and debris floating to earth—dreamily, almost ethereally—

the entire world muffled into silence. I looked up to see where Davos had stood but there was nothing there. Turning my head, I saw a bundle of clothing hanging on the bushes where Lèa had been, and fear gathered in my chest like a living thing.

"Lèa," I croaked, not recognizing my own voice.

"I am here," came her voice as if from very far away.

I let my head sag gently back to the ground as if it were too heavy to lift. She was alive. For now, that was enough.

"Jules!"

I wet my lips and heard Luc call my name. Again and again.

"I am here," I said, weakly, raising a hand

"Jules!" Another voice. This one full of fear and desperate hope.

Justine.

I lifted my head. From out of the corner of my eye I saw the world still slowly floating down around me. The space from where Justine had fallen was a pile of smoking rubble now.

"Luc! They are here!" Justine called. "Lèa! Lèa!"

The next thing I felt was Luc's arms around me.

"*Chérie*, you are alive," Luc said as if to confirm the fact to himself.

"Justine?" I asked.

"She is fine," he said, his voice close to my ear. "I caught her from below."

"And Lèa?" I asked, now struggling to a sitting position and looking around. A war zone.

Justine was kneeling near where Lèa sat. Lèa had been standing a good twenty yards further away from the blast zone than I. When I looked at her, she nodded and gave me a thumbs-up signal. I tried to remember if I'd ever seen her do that as long as I've known her. It was such an American thing to do. My eyes misted with emotion, and I nodded back at her.

"Davos?" I asked Luc.

We both turned to look at the spot where the man had last stood staring down at the grenade at his feet, trying to decide what to do. And like so many things in life, that decision had been made for him.

53

The beautiful autumn morning the twins got their medals had a crispness in the air that carried with it the scent of fallen leaves and woodsmoke. It told everyone at the ceremony more emphatically than words could that autumn would soon be upon us. I looked around at the transformed village square and smiled. Rows of white folding chairs were neatly arranged in the square, facing a small stage adorned with a garland of fresh flowers behind the war memorial. A large banner read, "Honoring Our Chabanel Heroes: A Grateful Country Remembers." Vibrant bunting in red, white, and blue crisscrossed between lampposts and rooftops, fluttering gently in the fall breeze. It was the perfect tableau of celebration and remembrance befitting the honor of watching *les soeurs* receive their credit for courage during the war years.

I sat between the twins who were dressed in their Sunday best and for two people who'd fought me as hard as they had from receiving this honor, they were doing a good job of behaving as if they might possibly believe they deserved all the accolades. Around us, the villagers of

Chabanel were a sea of familiar faces—Marie Fournier, amazingly not in a wheelchair, Matteo, Madame Gabin, Elise Lefèvre, Monsieurs Dubois and Dellaux and Thibault.

I hadn't seen Thibault much since Davos blew himself up, but he smiled at me from the back row where he sat with one of his greasy pals and I grinned back.

Everyone was dressed to the nines. Some ancient veterans were there, wearing their own medals, the ribbons frayed with time but worn with a dignified pride. The younger generation was present too, children dressed smartly with their hands clutching small flags provided by the local council and their expressions a mixture of boredom and awe.

I was glad to see the little ones looking at the sisters with such reverence. It was nice to think they'd look twice the next time they saw one of them doddering about the village and maybe remember what amazing women the sisters had been in their time. Only a few of us knew that they were still amazing.

Katrine sat with the government officials from Paris who would physically bestow the medals on the twins. I loved seeing Katrine up there on the dais looking all professional and in charge. It was a good look for her. I especially appreciated her mother and kids watching her from the front row. It did them good—especially Katrine's mother—to see Katrine in a position of respect and admiration.

I reached out and took each of the hands of the twins and waited while the ministers from Paris got ready for the presentation. I didn't look around for Luc. I knew he wasn't here. That made me sad, so I made a concentrated effort to block the thought from my mind. Today was a special day and not one for thinking of loss or regrets.

It had been three months since Davos tried to execute

the sisters and ended up killing himself instead. Since then, I've heard the whole story of how he forced the twins to go with him that day—he'd threatened to wait for me to come home and kill me too if they didn't willingly go with him.

As I watched Katrine get up and approach the podium, I gave each of the twins' hands a squeeze.

"Here we go," I whispered.

Something about that moment hit me in the gut, reminding me that despite my best efforts Luc should be here too. As hard as I tried not to, my thoughts drifted painfully back to my last conversation with him.

∽

It was one week after the showdown at the supply depot when I went to Luc's cottage so that we could finally talk. All the fanfare and paperwork about Hèlo's murder and what had happened at the supply depot site was over. Justine had sustained a hairline fracture to her elbow in the fall even though Luc had caught her from a level spot he'd located just below the ledge. Lèa was still having trouble hearing properly after the blast. But aside from all that, life had returned to normal.

The door to Luc's cottage was open, so I just walked in and found him standing in the center of his small living room amid a veritable mountain of packing boxes stacked high around the room. Dust motes danced in the shafts of light that spilled through the open windows, stirred by Luc's movements as he folded clothes before placing them into boxes.

I felt a stab of dismay. I gestured to all the boxes. He smiled ruefully at me. It was the first true smile I'd seen from him in months.

"I thought you said we'd have a chance to talk about steps going forward," I said as I took a seat at the kitchen table—the place where I had failed him so many times in the months of our marriage.

"I know," he said. "I'm still happy to talk."

He came to me and kissed me on the cheek before turning back to his work. Immediately I sensed the difference in him. Incredibly, and painfully—for me at least—he was at peace.

"But talking won't change your mind," I said.

"Does it surprise you?" he said. "We haven't been very good on the talking part of our marriage."

I swallowed down a lump in my throat.

"I thought I'd at least get a vote," I said.

"You can still vote."

"But your vote counts double."

He stopped then and dropped the pair of slacks he was folding to come sit down opposite me.

"I can't stay, Jules," he said sadly. "Nothing about staying feels right for me. I'm sorry. I'm not good at examining why that is. You of all people must know that. I only know how I feel."

I felt the heat behind my eyelids as I struggled not to let the tears out. The room, if not the whole world, felt for a moment like it was slowly spinning. In many ways I'd prayed for this moment. The moment when Luc finally knew how he felt about us. So, yay me! I finally got what I wished for.

Unfortunately, it's when he's in the process of walking out the door.

"Can't we just let it be for a while?" I asked. "Can't we just see where we go from here? Play it as it lays?"

He shook his head and looked into my eyes.

"People change," I said. "Down the road might be different for both of us. We'll be different."

He reached over and took my hand.

"I'll love you forever, Jules. That is the truth. I'll never stop wishing I was a different kind of man who could've made it work."

There wasn't much to say in response to that. It was clear he was determined to say goodbye. As I stood there listening to him, I thought of all the times we'd broken up before, all the times that we'd walked away from each other. I thought of how you can love someone with your whole heart and still not be able to live with him. And if we tried, we'd only be wearing each other out trying to change the other person. And end up hating each other. Maybe that was all true. But maybe it wasn't true forever. I guess I would just have to be patient to wait and see.

54

After the ceremony, once the village had applauded the twins until their hands were chapped, we all headed *en masse* toward the village hall for a reception for our honored guests.

I'm told the whole village pitched in to create the feast fit for honoring *les soeurs*. There were countless plates of *foie gras*, grilled duck and lobster, pots of beef burgundy, and of course an endless supply of breads and pastries. Naturally, all the breads—*fougasse, baguettes, croissants* and *pains aux chocolat*—were handmade by our own Marie Fournier—although I'm not sure they would've been if she'd known how close to the top of my suspects list she'd been in Hèlo's murder case. Speaking of Hèlo, there was also a satisfying representation of cheeses capped off by two large wheels of Banon, compliments of Thibault. Also on the groaning tables of food were framed photographs and mementos from the war years displayed on easels which provided a visual journey through the sisters' lives and the village's history.

"Are you finally happy now?" Lèa asked me in a long-suffering voice although the National Order of Merit medal was pinned proudly to the lapel of her best Sunday dress.

"Yep," I said. "Thank you for letting me do this. It meant a lot."

She gave a sigh as if to say it had been a real personal trial for her, but I happened to know she was proud to finally have the recognition for the things she'd done in the war. The fact that she'd only recently had to fight another villain in the name of that same war seemed to underscore for her the validity of the medal she now wore. In a strange way I feel beholding to Davos for that. If he hadn't come to Chabanel breathing all his excitement and passion about the war and the people who'd fought in it—and that part of his dedication was absolutely genuine—I never would've made the effort to reach out to the national government to make sure the twins were recognized before they died.

The very air itself seemed to buzz with effervescence of both the bubbly everyone was drinking and the celebration itself. As I looked around, I couldn't remember the community hall looking more festive nor filled as it was today with more people.

It felt strange to be here without Luc. In his own way, he'd contributed to this moment, and I hated that he wasn't here to celebrate it with all of us. I spotted Madame Gabin loaded down with a massive pile of *foie gras* and *boeuf bourguignon* on her plate, talking with her mouth full to one of the villagers, imparting or taking in whatever juicy village news there was to be had. I also saw Matteo on the perimeter of the room. Our eyes met. He scowled and looked away.

I didn't blame him for being angry. One of the things Luc did before he resigned his position was to put my name up for the position of acting Chief of Police. A month later, the village rubber-stamped the suggestion. Since then, there has been more than one time when the idea has hit me hard that the very thing Luc feared would happen actually happened. I'd replaced him. I don't believe I'll do the job better than he did. I'll probably do it differently. Because I am not a French national, I have to travel to Lyons once a week for two days of police training. When I am done, I still won't be an official French police officer, but I'll be qualified for the job I am already doing—acting chief of police.

I've officially moved back into *La Fleurette* with the twins and allowed Luc's cottage to be used by a young couple who were recently married and needed a place to live. I truly wished them more luck there than Luc and I had, and I won't say it doesn't sting every time I drive by on my way to work. (Oh, yeah, I have a car now.)

I glanced again at Matteo, but he was deliberately not looking at me. I knew I'd have my hands full with him. As I understood the parameters of my new job, I wouldn't have the power to fire him—and he knew it. I was going to have to find a way to work with him.

"Don't you worry about Matteo," Katrine said as she walked over to me with two champagne glasses in her hands.

I grinned and took one. Thibault was behind her with his own glass. He and Katrine lifted their glasses to me.

"There's a new sheriff in town," Thibault said with a wink.

I laughed and sipped from my glass as Katrine held hers up for yet another toast.

"To Jules," she said. "For making our little village her home and for helping to transform every one of us for the better."

"Hear! Hear!" Thibault said and drank again.

I smiled at Katrine. I would need every ounce of her support in the coming months if I was going to pull off being the ex-pat American police chief of Chabanel.

"What is happening?" Lèa said as she and Justine joined our group.

"Just congratulating the good and the fortunate," Katrine said, raising her glass to the twins.

"Congratulations, *nos héroïnes*," Thibault said lifting his glass to them too.

We all toasted a few more times—to the village of Chabanel, to Luc wherever he was, to all the people who had put together the feast, to our illustrious mayor, and to the government officials who'd come down from Paris for today's ceremony.

As I watched the people I loved surround me—each of them flushed with happiness as well as champagne—I found myself feeling a profound sense of gratitude for what I had, in spite of what I'd lost.

Honestly, it was a distinction I was quite proud I was able to make.

∽

Be sure to look for *Crepe Expectaions*, *Book 11 of The Stranded in Provence Mysteries.*

ABOUT THE AUTHOR

USA TODAY Bestselling Author Susan Kiernan-Lewis is the author of *The Maggie Newberry Mysteries,* the post-apocalyptic thriller series *The Irish End Games, The Mia Kazmaroff Mysteries, The Stranded in Provence Mysteries, The Claire Baskerville Mysteries,* and *The Savannah Time Travel Mysteries.*

Visit www.susankiernanlewis.com or follow Author Susan Kiernan-Lewis on Facebook.

Printed in Great Britain
by Amazon